*Before she thought about it once,
let alone twice, she threw her arms
around him and gave him a huge hug.*

In response, Dillon's arms went around her.

Their enthusiastic embrace turned into something else when she raised her gaze to his. She could feel his muscles under his suit coat go taut. More than that, she felt his body heat, smelled his aftershave and fell into the golden-brown of his eyes. Whenever she was within touching distance of Dillon, her whole world changed. It became brighter, clearer, more adventurous. It was a no-holds-barred feeling that she could do anything, or be anything. It was so crazy, yet—

"Do you want another kiss as much as I do?" he asked, his voice husky.

"Yes," Erika breathed, waiting, anticipating, knowing she shouldn't be doing this but unable to help herself because it felt so right.

Dear Reader,

I've come to several crossroads in my life that could have changed the course of it—what job I accepted, an engagement, a marriage proposal, the decision to start a family. My hero, Dillon Traub, is at a crossroads. Because of past decisions which he now considers mistakes, he wants to take his time choosing a new career path. But love doesn't wait and can't be predicted or even managed! When he meets Erika, a single mom, his past wounds are opened. What he comes to realize is that true love can not only heal the past but point the way to the future.

I'm honored to be part of the MONTANA MAVERICKS continuity series. I hope you enjoy reading about Dillon and Erika as much as I enjoyed writing about them!

All my best,

Karen Rose Smith

FROM DOCTOR...
TO DADDY

KAREN ROSE SMITH

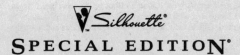

SPECIAL EDITION

Published by Silhouette Books

America's Publisher of Contemporary Romance

Special thanks and acknowledgment to
Karen Rose Smith for her contribution to the
MONTANA MAVERICKS:
THUNDER CANYON COWBOYS continuity.

 SILHOUETTE BOOKS

Recycling programs
for this product may
not exist in your area.

ISBN-13: 978-0-373-65547-2

FROM DOCTOR...TO DADDY

Visit Silhouette Books at www.eHarlequin.com

Printed in U.S.A.

Books by Karen Rose Smith

KAREN ROSE SMITH

Award-winning and bestselling author Karen Rose Smith has seen more than sixty-five of her novels published since 1991. Living in Pennsylvania with her husband—who was her college sweetheart—and their two cats, she has been writing full-time since the start of her career. She enjoys researching and visiting the West and Southwest, where this series of books is set. Readers can receive updates on Karen's latest releases and write to her through her Web site at www.karenrosesmith.com or at P.O. Box 1545, Hanover, PA 17331.

To my dad—
I'll always remember building model ships,
rolling a red scooter, playing blackjack and
riding my bike the day you removed the training wheels.
I miss you.

Chapter One

The door to Dr. Dillon Traub's office at the infirmary in the lodge suddenly flew open. A tall, husky man carrying a boy of about eight rushed inside. "You've got to do something, Doc. I can't find his EpiPen."

Erika Rodriguez was right on the man's heels. "This is Dave Lindstrom. He thinks his son Jeff is having a reaction to something he ate." Her words were quick and precise, yet she seemed calm.

As Dillon rose from his desk, their gazes collided and the zing he'd been experiencing ever since he'd met his receptionist hit him full force. Even now.

Pushing aside any thoughts other than those about this little boy, Dillon took Jeff into his own arms and ran into a well-equipped exam room. "Call 9-1-1," he shot over his shoulder at Erika, experiencing the gut-wrenching ache he always felt when he was near a child in crisis…remembering his own child.

"I already did," Erika called after him.

An internist, Dillon could handle almost any emergency that cropped up at Thunder Canyon Resort. Marshall Cates—the resident doctor here—had assured him not many emergencies occurred at the resort.

So much for Marshall's assurances.

The boy's breathing was labored and his lips were blue and swelling. Dillon knew he had everything he needed to reverse the reaction if it wasn't too late.

Too late, echoed in his mind, as it often had over the past few years.

It wouldn't be too late for *this* child.

"Hold on, Jeff," Dillon said in a low voice as he laid the boy on the table.

Expertly assessing Jeff's height, weight and condition, Dillon grabbed an EpiPen with the appropriate dosage from the medicine cabinet. Instants later, he'd administered it, pulled over the oxygen tank and let Jeff breathe it in through the nasal cannula. Erika assisted any way she could while Dillon ran an IV line. All the while, he monitored the little boy's pulse, checked his breathing, comforted him in low tones and prayed for the anaphylactic reaction to reverse.

Dillon was aware of Erika beside him. He'd been *too* aware of her since he'd briefly met her on his vacation here in June. When he'd accepted Marshall Cates's offer to take over as staff doctor for the month of September while Marshall was away, Grant Clifton, the resort's manager, had assigned Erika to be his receptionist. Since then, Dillon's awareness of her had revved up into something even more disturbing—desire. He hadn't felt *real* desire since well before his divorce.

Erika had never had any medical training but seemed able to take on any assignment she was given with a competence that made her a valued employee in Grant's eyes, especially given the recent budget cuts. Those same budget cuts had made it necessary for Ruthann, Marshall's nurse, to come on duty when Dillon went off. Not that he was really ever off. He was usually on call twenty-four hours a day, except for the odd night when the retired physician in town would cover for him.

Now Erika suddenly glanced toward the hallway, her long dark brown, wavy hair sliding over her shoulder. "I hear the sirens. The paramedics are coming."

Standing at the boy's shoulder, Jeff's father murmured, "Thank God."

Dillon checked Jeff's nailbeds and was relieved to see the blue was receding. His lips were less swollen and pinker, too. "I know you're scared, Jeff," he said clasping the child's arm. "But everything's going to be okay."

Jeff's hazel eyes darted to Dillon's face.

"You can breathe easier now, can't you?"

Jeff nodded, then reached his hand out for his dad who took it and squeezed it tightly. The husky man's brow was beaded with sweat and he looked as if emotion was choking his throat. Finally he managed to say, "He's all I have."

Dillon reached out his hand to the lodge's guest. "Mr. Lindstrom, I'm Dr. Traub. I'll follow along to the hospital to make sure all goes smoothly as soon as I give my nurse a call so she can cover."

"I'll call her," Erika offered. "She's due in soon, so she's probably around the resort."

Erika moved away from Dillon's side, her figure trim in her navy suit. Her skirt was just the right length to be professional and her white silky blouse had a scooped neckline that showed off her beautiful olive skin.

As she passed him, her scent, light and tempting, enveloped him. She turned her head and her dark eyes stayed on his. For a moment, a rippling intensity skittered back and forth between them.

She broke eye contact and had almost reached the door when Dillon caught the sound of voices and the clang of a gurney. All at once, there the paramedics were—ready to handle an emergency...ready to take care of Jeff while they transported him to the hospital.

Dillon was so grateful that Erika's calm handling of the crisis, as well as his ministrations, had saved Jeff's life. He wished recovery was an outcome for every sick child.

Yet he knew firsthand it wasn't. He'd lost his own child to leukemia—and there hadn't been a damn thing he could do about it.

At her desk, Erika suddenly went on alert a few hours later. She recognized the bootfalls of Dr. Dillon Traub as he strode up the hall to the infirmary.

She had heard he was the heir of an oil fortune. Western-cut suits that impeccably fit his broad shoulders, fine leather boots, as well as the oil fortune were all good reasons to stay away from him. Ever since she'd met him in June and chemistry had rippled between them, she'd known becoming involved with him would be trouble.

Not to worry, she reassured herself. She was sure he wouldn't be interested in her at all if he knew the truth about her.

Now as Dillon appeared in the doorway to the infirmary suite's reception area, Erika noticed his tawny blond hair looked as if he'd run his fingers through it. It had a wave that styling couldn't deny.

He wasn't smiling, and she worried that Jeff had taken a turn for the worse. "Is Jeff okay?"

Dillon's gaze held hers. "He's doing great. And I also want to tell you that you handled yourself and the emergency very well. But we've got a problem. Mr. Lindstrom's talking about suing the resort."

Dillon's praise meant a lot. *Simply because she wanted a promotion,* she assured herself. "Suing the resort? Why?" she asked.

Crossing to her desk, Dillon stopped at the corner. "The kitchen has been making Jeff special meals because of his food allergies. Jeff said he ate his lunch right before the attack. Mr. Lindstrom is convinced there was a nut residue in the salad. He assured me he has enough money to keep the resort tied up in lawsuits for years."

"Does he want a settlement?"

"I don't think so. I think he just wants to make sure it doesn't happen to anyone else."

"But if he sues the resort—"

"I know. These are tough times. Resort reservations are down considerably, especially for September. I'll have to speak with Grant about the possible lawsuit."

Erika noticed the deepened lines around Dillon's eyes and didn't believe the lawsuit was the only matter pressing on him. "Jeff won't have aftereffects from today, will he?"

"I hope not."

Was that pain in Dillon's eyes? Turmoil? About what?

She broke eye contact, feeling the flutter in her tummy that happened whenever Dillon was around. She instinctively knew if she kept gazing into his eyes, almost anything could happen. She couldn't *let* anything happen. After Scott Spencerman had left her so suddenly she'd made a plan for her life—and it didn't involve romance. She would *not* be distracted no matter what the gossips said about her.

Putting the brakes on the course of their conversation, Dillon reached across the desk and tapped the notepad in front of her, obviously wanting to change the subject. She'd doodled guitars and cowboy hats and a pair of boots.

"What's this?"

"I was just trying to decide what to do next." Should she confide in Dillon Traub? Why not? This wasn't anything personal. After the gossip fest the town had participated in about her, she kept everything personal away from her professional life.

"It's Frontier Days," she admitted.

In addition to being a receptionist to Dillon—which wasn't always a very busy position—she was managing the Frontier Days Festival scheduled for the fourth weekend in September. The festival had been planned to boost business for the town and resort. It was a huge project for her, but Grant Clifton had said he had confidence in her abilities. She was hoping to use the festival to score a much-needed promotion. If she could be promoted from receptionist to even guest-room manager, she'd have more to spend on her monthly budget...more to save for Emilia's future.

"Problems?"

"For the most part, everything is falling in line. I feel I have a handle on events in town as well as guest-stay enhancements here. There's just one element that's missing and I can't seem to do anything about it."

"What's that?"

"The entertainment. I wanted to have a really great

draw, like a well-known country singer—Brad Paisley, Keith Urban, Zane Gunther. I've called every manager I could find. I even have the county arena at the fairgrounds lined up for that Saturday night. But I don't have a star to perform there."

Dillon said, "Maybe I can help you with that."

"Do you know someone?" she asked with surprise.

"I might." His smile was a bit mysterious and, oh, so sexy.

She went on, "I'm a little worried about the weather, too."

He was actually listening. That wasn't a trait she had found in many men. "It can be unpredictable in September. I'm not planning summer activities in case the weather turns colder. Still, tourists will be in and out of the stores, sampling food from the chili booths, listening to campaign speeches with a lot more enthusiasm if we're having Indian summer. I've made alternative plans for everything, but the best laid plans…"

Dillon had seemed to relax and now sat casually on the corner of her desk. "The resort needs tourists before the ski season starts to fill vacancies and the town needs them to support Thunder Canyon businesses."

"That's why I planned Frontier Days for late in the month. The candidates for mayor seemed pleased with that, too, so they could rev up their campaigns for the November election."

"You've thought of everything."

She felt color rising from her neck to her cheeks. "Not really."

Electricity crackled in the air as they gazed into each other's eyes.

"Is Ruthann here?" Dillon asked, seemingly out of the blue.

"She's back in her office."

He nodded. "I'll check in with her before I leave for my dinner break. How would you like to get a bite to eat with me?"

It was after five and technically Erika was finished for the day. She had responsibilities at home but with a phone call to her mom...

She was so tempted by Dillon's offer. For the past three years, she'd shunned dating and steered clear of men. No man had ever made her heart race like Dillon did, not even Scott Spencerman. Was that a good or bad thing? She'd fallen for Scott's charming flattery, as well as his suave, sophisticated persona.

Dillon didn't seem to give idle compliments. He just—

Made her feel like a woman? Made her feel alive? Made her feel as if she were missing something?

What harm could one dinner do? No one could gossip about that, could they? And it might be a test to see just what kind of man Dillon was. Whether he could enjoy beer and a country jukebox...if he would mind being seen with his receptionist in public. "How about the Hitching Post in town?"

"The Hitching Post is fine with me," he offered with a smile that could easily curl her toes if she let it. He was one sexy, attractive Texan with that defined jaw, golden-brown eyes and sandy-blond hair. Yet he didn't seem to be a player. He had confidence but not the arrogance some men emanated when they thought they could hook any woman they crooked their finger at.

Erika was about to confirm their date, when Stacy Gillette appeared in the doorway. A pretty brunette, Stacy was one of the social directors at the resort. She was lithe and friendly and always seemed to have a smile. But then Erika supposed Stacy didn't have a reputation to repair or something to prove.

Dillon's face lit up when he saw the social director. "Hi, Stacy. I haven't seen you around since I arrived. I was hoping we'd connect." He gave Stacy a huge hug and a light kiss.

That kiss and his familiarity with the social director bothered Erika and she knew it shouldn't.

Turning to Erika, Dillon said, "I met Stacy in Thunder Canyon when I was a kid."

Stacy was beaming, too, as if seeing Dillon was the highlight of her day. She merely nodded to Erika, acknowledging her. Erika didn't have many friends on staff because of the gossip that had followed her...and the friends she'd lost. She didn't want to confide anything to a fellow employee that could be used against her. The one friend she'd made recently at the resort was Erin Castro, a newcomer to Thunder Canyon. Erika felt comfortable with her, probably because the woman knew nothing of Erika's checkered past.

Stacy addressed Dillon. "I thought I'd drop by and if you were still here, see if you wanted to go to dinner."

"I have a commitment tonight," he said, without glancing at Erika, even though she hadn't given him a final answer yet. "How about tomorrow?"

"That sounds great," Stacy agreed. She gave his arm a playful jab. "Then you can catch me up on what the great doctor's been doing in Midland, Texas...besides working. I won't keep you. See you tomorrow," she said, then with a wave and with another flashing smile, she was gone.

Dillon's gaze returned to Erika's. "I do have a commitment tonight, don't I?"

Were he and Stacy simply childhood friends? Or did he date more than one woman at a time?

One meal. She could see if he really *was* a regular guy. Or if he was a player like Scott had turned out to be.

"Yes," she answered, rolling her chair away from her desk. "I'll gather my things and meet you at the Hitching Post."

Straightening, he nodded. "See you there."

Erika hoped to high heaven she wouldn't regret getting to know Dr. Dillon Traub just a little better.

Erika opened the door to the Hitching Post and stepped inside, troubled by her phone conversation with her mom. When Erika had told her she was having a bite to eat with Dr. Traub, the cold silence had reminded Erika of too many things she'd like to forget.

Erika had assured her, "It's just a bite to eat," and explained about the emergency with Jeff. Still, her mom's attitude had been more than a little concerned and Erika knew why. After all, her romance with Scott had put them both through the wringer.

At twenty-three, she'd been working as a receptionist in a real-estate office in town. Scott had bought one of the condos at Thunder Canyon Resort and intended to spend his spare time there. She'd spent spare time there with him, believing she was totally in love. He'd been handsome and polished, and she'd fallen for him hook, line and sinker. She should have had a clue when he didn't particularly want to be seen in public with her. But red flags hadn't been on her mind—only the bliss she'd felt in his arms.

She'd never forget the expression on his face when she'd told him...

She sighed, wishing the past could stay in the past. He'd used her and discarded her, and her mother had helped pick up the pieces. Erika would never forget any of it, nor the whispers that she'd been looking for a way up in life…that Scott was her ticket and she was a gold digger.

Since then, she'd made sure her behavior had been impeccable.

But now here she was, having dinner with eligible— and rich—Dillon Traub. Maybe her mother was right to be concerned. Maybe a simple dinner *could* cause more gossip she didn't want to deal with.

The Hitching Post's flavor hit Erika as soon as she stepped inside. There was a beautiful walnut bar to her right, packed with diners jockeying for tables or finishing their happy-hour conversations. When she'd suggested the place to Dillon, she'd forgotten about that painting of Lily Devine above the bar. She'd been painted almost nude, except for a bit of diaphanous cloth. What had Erika been thinking?

She'd been thinking that maybe the beer, peanuts and honky-tonk music would distract her from the chemistry she felt between them.

When she spotted him at a back table, her heartbeats tripped over each other. In his suit, he stood out. Most everyone here was dressed casually. But something about his appearance was different and she suddenly realized what it was. He'd discarded his bolo tie and opened the collar of his shirt. Hot enough in his fine suit, that open collar made him look worldly and, oh, so sexy. Hello. She'd already known she was attracted to him, but now attraction took on a whole new meaning.

She'd have something to eat and be gone.

When she reached the table, he smiled and she

couldn't help but smile back. Although formality was
left at the door at the Hitching Post, she was momentarily charmed when Dillon pulled out her chair for
her. As he bent to push it in, she caught the scent of his
cologne and her heart skipped a beat.

Don't fall for good manners, she chided herself. *Or
chemistry.*

After they were both seated, the table for two seem-
ing much too intimate despite the other patrons around
them, Dillon said, "The waitress came around but I
didn't know what you wanted." He raised his hand and
caught a server's attention.

A redhead with a long ponytail hurried over. "Ready
now?" she asked enthusiastically, eyeing Dillon.

Dillon motioned for Erika to go first and she ordered
cola with a twist of lime. She needed caffeine for the
long night ahead. Dillon ordered soda, too, instead of
something with liquor. Then she remembered that he
was on call. So much for the see-if-he-likes-beer test.

Country music blared from the jukebox and a few
of the patrons had started a line dance. Dillon smiled
again. "I never could get the hang of that. I think I have
two left feet."

"But you've tried it?"

"Oh, sure. Country's big in Texas, too."

She blushed. She should have realized that. "Do you
like country?"

"Some. I like jazz, Nickelback and Paul McCartney,
too."

And so the conversation went as they ordered, waited
a short time and then enjoyed their meals. Knowing a
big meal would make her sleepy and that was the last
thing she needed, she ordered a taco salad. But Dillon

dug into his ribs and coleslaw like an enthusiast. His plate was empty before she'd finished.

He wiped his mouth with his napkin and tossed it down beside his plate. "I've got to admit, the ribs here are good, but D.J.'s are better."

Dillon's cousin D.J. Traub owned the Rib Shack, located near the lodge. Actually, he not only owned the Rib Shack at the resort, but other Rib Shacks across the U.S. From what she knew of D.J. and his brother, Dax, they hadn't come from wealth. They'd both found their niche and made the most of it. She wasn't going to hide the fact that she knew Dillon was indeed more than a doctor.

"Tell me why you went into medicine," she requested. "From the rumors I've heard, you could have been CEO of the company your father started."

He arched a brow, but didn't look upset or annoyed at her question. "There are a ton of reasons why I wasn't the one to manage Traub Oil Industries. My mother took over the business after Dad died. My brother Ethan is the CFO now and he fits the part."

There was obviously a story there, but Dillon didn't seem about to confide in her. Of course, they didn't know each other all that well, so why would he?

However, he surprised her when he added, "My father died on an oil rig when I was twelve. He took a fall and his injuries were serious. Even as a twelve-year-old, I wondered if I had been a doctor, could I have saved him? That's the reason I went into medicine."

She was remembering more details she'd heard about Dax and D.J. Traub and didn't know if she was stepping into dangerous territory. But Dillon had opened the door.

"Your cousins—didn't their mom die when they were kids?"

"How I forget the gossip mill in Thunder Canyon," Dillon remarked with a rueful smile. "No one's history is private. To answer your question—yes. I think that was one of the reasons we were close, even though I only saw them summers when we were growing up. We shared a difficult experience, and I guess it created a bond between us."

A country ballad began playing on the jukebox. Dillon nodded to the familiar melody. "I think this conversation's gotten a little serious. Would you like to dance? I can slow dance much better than I can line dance."

She hesitated, knowing she should say no. But the urge to feel like a desirable woman again was strong. "Yes, I would," she replied.

Before she could rise to her feet, he was behind her chair, helping her up. He definitely was a gentleman... *or* a good pretender.

The dance floor was crowded and that made her feel more comfortable for some reason. No one she knew was in sight.

She had to admit that she'd imagined Dillon holding her. But the real deal was something else entirely. As soon as his arm went around her and his large hand took hers, she knew she was indeed in trouble. He was at least six inches taller than she was—the top of her head just came to his nose. In his arms she could feel the strength of his muscles. Did he work out? At dinner he'd told her he tried to go riding many mornings. To top it all off, at this time of day, his jawline was becoming slightly stubbly. The scruffier look suited him.

When she looked up and her gaze collided with his interested brown eyes, nerves in her body tingled—nerves that she didn't even know she had.

Too much…too soon…too fast.

After taking a deep breath, she eased away from him slightly to start another conversation. It was the only way she could distract herself from what was going on in her body, let alone the fantasies in her mind. He didn't try to hold her close, but kept his eyes on hers as she moved away. Those few inches mattered a lot. She could breathe a little easier. And think. What was wrong with her tonight? She'd been so calm and cool-headed ever since Scott.

"You said your mom took over your dad's business," she began. "I think that's wonderful."

"Lots of men in the company didn't share your opinion, but she made it clear they either had to come aboard with the program or they'd be gone."

"How many brothers and sisters do you have?"

"I have four brothers and one sister."

"Wow! Your mom handled all of you and a career, too?"

His silence told her this wasn't a question he was comfortable with, yet he didn't duck it. "Two years after my dad died, my mom remarried. Peter was working on the rig when my dad fell. He helped her through all of it and they got close."

His hand ruffled through the waves on her shoulders and she wondered if he did it to distract her. If he did, he was succeeding. "Today's the first time you've worn your hair down," he noticed.

When she kept it tied back or in a chignon, she felt more professional. But this morning, she'd been running late. "I was a bit rushed this morning so I let nature take its course."

As soon as the words were out of her mouth, she wanted to recall them. Nature. Attraction between a man and a woman was exactly what was going on here. They both knew it.

Dillon's thumb played teasingly against hers. The sensual sensation raised her temperature a couple of notches.

So she tried again with conversation. "Are you planning to spend much time with your cousins, now that you're here again?"

"Back to that, are we?" he asked teasingly.

"I'm just curious. There are so many stories floating around about Dax and D.J., their feud, their fistfight, the women they married. Were you part of all that?"

"No, I wasn't. I was busy establishing my practice."

Again something that she couldn't decipher passed over his expression.

But he continued, "We did have a family reunion in June and we had a great time."

"Do they have children?" She shouldn't have asked, but she might as well know where he stood on that subject.

A shadow crossed Dillon's face. "Dax has a six-year-old and a two-year-old. D.J.'s little boy is two, also. I haven't been around them much. But I'm looking forward to some time with them while I'm here."

Dillon's tone didn't match his words. He was being polite about it.

Erika's blood felt like ice water. All she could think was that he was another man who didn't like responsibility. He was another man who thought fatherhood would be a burden. He was another man who would be a mistake if she saw him again.

What was she doing here with Dillon Traub?

For the rest of the dance, she didn't look him in the eye. She pretended he could be any one of the men on the dance floor—no one special, no one sexy, no one who made her heart beat much too fast.

When the song ended, Erika was relieved, but Dillon didn't let her pull away. "What's wrong?" he asked.

"I just remembered—" No, she wasn't going to make an excuse. She wasn't going to lie to him. "I have to go, Dillon. Thanks for dinner but I do have to go."

Then she left him standing there, looking puzzled as she walked away. And when she pushed open the door into the cool September air, she didn't look back. Her daughter Emilia came first.

And she would never forget that.

Chapter Two

Dillon pulled money from his wallet and flicked it onto the table with his bill. What had gone wrong with Erika?

Just as he asked himself the question, he felt the vibration of his cell phone on his belt. Did someone at the resort need him?

When he pulled the phone from its holder, he checked the screen and smiled. "Hold on a sec, Corey, until I leave the restaurant."

Outside the door, Dillon took a deep breath, wondering why Erika's leaving had disappointed him so deeply. He didn't even know her. He shouldn't even think about knowing her. He was here for a month, then he'd be gone. Besides that, she had to be twelve or thirteen years younger than he was. Maybe that was the whole problem. She decided she'd rather be out with someone her own age.

Now, however, his mind went to his brother, holding the line from Midland, Texas. "Okay, now I can hear," Dillon said. "I was at the Hitching Post. You know how noisy that can get."

Corey laughed, a good old Texas chuckle. At thirty-three and six feet tall, with light brown hair and brown eyes, his brother was the epitome of a Texas male. As a management consultant, he dressed stylishly when he chose to, but he was most at home in his boots and jeans. He'd spent some time with Dillon, their cousins and friends at the Hitching Post in June.

"What were you doing at the Hitching Post?" Corey asked. "Don't tell me you were trying to pick up somebody at happy hour?"

Corey enjoyed women's company and didn't understand why Dillon still didn't date.

He and his brother had always been honest with each other. Although Ethan was between them in age, Corey and Dillon thought more alike on subjects *other* than women and had gotten to be better friends the older they'd grown.

So now when Corey asked, Dillon was honest. "I was here with someone."

There was a pause as if Corey was thinking about that. "With someone? Like the receptionist you met at the resort this summer?"

"You guessed that *how?*"

"I saw the way you looked at her when she led us to Marshall's office in June. But more than that, I saw the way she looked back."

"Yeah, well, she's not looking back now. We were having an enjoyable evening, then all of a sudden she froze up and left. I would have appreciated a hint as to what I did wrong."

"You'll probably never know," Corey empathized. "I don't understand women any more than you do. They have a language I don't get—a language they want us to learn, yet they don't want to teach it to us."

After another pause, Dillon asked, "Did you call just to see how things are going here?"

"Partly. Actually I might be in Montana again in November. I'm thinking about staying at the lodge. How do you like it there?"

"It's luxurious. Anything you might need is at your fingertips."

"But?" Corey asked perceptively.

"But if you're going to stay any length of time, you might want to rent one of the condos. Many of them are empty."

"Thanks—I'll keep that in mind. So how do you like Marshall's practice?"

"A medical practice like this one could be any doctor's lifelong dream. I can even glimpse elk from the wall of windows in my office."

"Yet it's not *your* dream?"

"I can't dream anymore, Corey."

The silence between them was telling and Dillon asked a clipped, "What?"

"You have to let go of the guilt. You'll never be happy again if you don't. For the millionth time, you had no control over Toby's leukemia."

"I don't want to talk about it." Thoughts of Dillon's four-and-a-half-year-old son who'd died were so bittersweet he usually closed the door on them.

"All right. So let's talk about what you're going to do when your stint for Marshall is up. Are you going to accept that concierge practice in Odessa?"

The doctor who had offered Dillon the position had

put a sweet deal on the table. "I don't know. Taking care of the guests at the resort is a somewhat similar experience. I'm going to see how I like it before I make up my mind."

"Good idea. The truth is I don't know if I can see you being at the beck and call of patients because they're paying you well for the opportunity to have you as their doctor. It doesn't sound like you."

"I never thought I'd be here at the resort, taking over for Marshall, either."

Corey waited a beat before asking, "So you just ran into this receptionist again?"

"Not exactly. Erika's my receptionist now."

"Ah-hah! The plot thickens. Just how did she come to *be* your receptionist?"

"Grant assigned her. I'm not taking up all her time. It's pretty slow for her most days, but she's the one planning Frontier Days. She's working right outside my office all day, so we interact."

"I see. And tonight you decided to interact on a personal rather than business level?"

His brother's words brought back the image of him holding Erika in his arms, his hand under her hair, his other hand clasping hers. At first, as they'd danced, she'd been close enough to arouse him. But then she'd needed some space. He got that. They didn't know each other very well. But leaving as she had—

"Ask her," Corey suggested.

"Ask her what?"

"Ask her why she left. That's what you want to know, right? Maybe she's one of those rare women who will actually tell you the truth."

His silence was answer enough for Corey.

His brother offered, "Yeah, the Texas Traubs inherited

as much pride as oil money. You know what Mom's always preached—pride comes before the fall. I think that means if you don't give up the pride, you're going to trip over something."

Purposely changing the subject again, Dillon asked, "Did you attend the family dinner on Sunday?"

"Oh, yeah. Peter was in great form, filling us all in verbatim on the latest board meeting."

"After all these years, we should realize Peter's not going to change," Dillon reminded his brother.

When their mother had married Peter Wexler, Dillon hadn't known what to think. At fourteen, he was still grieving for his dad and couldn't imagine another man moving into his father's place. His mother had told them she needed help with six kids and running a business. Peter knew the business from the ground up and she'd teach him what he didn't know.

Dillon had heard the gossip at school as she'd dated Peter, then married him. The grapevine had debated over whether or not he was a gold digger. People assumed the oil-rig foreman would take Claudia Traub's money and leave her high and dry...but first he'd share the good life with her. Since Dillon hadn't been about to accept *anyone* sitting in his father's chair at the table, he'd rebelled big-time. He'd stayed away from Peter as much as he could, making sure he participated in after-school sports, studied someplace other than home and spent summers with his cousins in Montana. He'd told himself constantly he only had to live through four years because then he'd be in college and on his own. He and Peter had settled into a kind of truce, but they'd never become close, never become son and father.

Away from all of it now, Dillon finally answered Corey's question.

"We all have our own lives now. He's always seemed to make Mom happy and that's what's important, right?" Dillon asked, still trying to convince himself.

"I guess," Corey agreed. After a pensive pause, he asked, "So what are you going to do about Erika?"

"Maybe I'll just do what you said and ask her why she left."

"Sounds like a plan."

"I'll talk to you soon," Dillon said.

Dillon attached his phone to his belt and strode to his sedan. Did he really want to find out why Erika had left? Why even bother when by the end of September, he'd be gone?

Early the next morning, Erika exited the women's locker room at the resort's gym dressed in her tank top, shorts and sneakers. She was a little out of sorts. For some reason, today it had been difficult to drop off Emilia at the neighborhood day care—her little girl hadn't wanted her to leave. Plus, her dinner with Dillon last night had stirred up pre–Scott Spencerman dreams—dreams of vows, shared goals and most of all children who brought such joy to everyday life. Yet Dillon had squashed them with his lack of enthusiasm for children…the dark emotion in his eyes when she'd mentioned his cousin's kids.

Erika stopped short when she spied the object of her thoughts. Last night, Dillon had told her he liked to go horseback riding. But the weather was damp and rainy today, so he must have opted for the workout room instead. She wished she could just walk by him and forget last night had ever happened. But essentially, he was her boss and she couldn't.

He had spotted her, too.

He'd finished with one of the weight stations. Grabbing a towel from a nearby bench, he slung it around his neck.

She swallowed hard. His broad shoulders and slim waist told her he'd always been an athlete. He was wearing a gray T-shirt with the sleeves cut off and navy gym shorts that didn't hide his powerful thigh muscles. There was a dark patch of sweat on his chest and under his arms. His body glistened from his workout, but he didn't seem self-conscious about it, though he wasn't smiling now as they both took a few steps toward each other.

"I didn't expect to see you here this morning," he commented.

"I come in a few times each week."

"I thought I'd save my favorite horse a wet, muddy ride."

She might as well jump into it. "I'm sorry I didn't pay my half of the bill last night. If you'd like—"

"Don't be silly. I asked you to dinner, remember?"

Oh, she remembered. Glancing at his body again, feeling heat creep through hers, she recalled exactly why she'd accepted his invitation.

"Did I say something to make you run off?"

He was direct, that was for sure, and she liked that about him. She liked too many things. "It wasn't you, Dillon. Really."

"That's hard to believe."

When she didn't say more, he took another step closer, and now they were within touching distance. "You have circles under your eyes." He gently touched one of them with his thumb.

Erika trembled and she hoped he couldn't feel it. She'd *never* felt this kind of chemistry before. Taking a shaky breath, she decided just to give him a little bit of personal information. "I was up late last night studying. I'm taking an online management course. After all, I don't want to be a receptionist forever."

"So you raced home to study?" He sounded…surprised. Maybe even a little impressed. "Would you like to do something like manage this whole resort someday?"

"Yes, I would. From everything I've seen here, I think I'd enjoy hotel management. I'm hoping that if I do a great job with Frontier Days, I'll be promoted."

Dillon's gaze passed over her assessingly as if he was taking stock of her appearance and her intelligence, maybe even her age. Her shoulders squared and she knew she raised her chin, wondering what was coming next. Dillon had always been a gentleman, but they were alone here. Scott had taken advantage of any time they were alone to make a move on her.

But Dillon didn't engage in idle flattery, nor did he step closer. He asked, "Do you want to stay in Thunder Canyon or move on?"

"I haven't thought about leaving." After all, she had a child and a life to make. "Why do you ask?"

"Because you're young, intelligent and beautiful. The whole world is open to you. Have you traveled at all?"

She shook her head.

"Do you want to?"

"Maybe some day, but now I have to make a living and I'm establishing roots. After all, this is where I was born and raised. Don't you feel that way about where you came from?"

He shrugged. "I think a career path can lead away from roots. If you want to become a resort manager, you could end up on a tropical island."

Maybe he felt as if he'd shared too much personal

information with her last night because he hadn't answered her question. "I can't picture myself leaving Montana. I feel grounded here." She knew that mostly had to do with her mother and her daughter, but he didn't need to know that. "Have you traveled much?" she asked, curious about his life...curious about what being wealthy meant.

"I traveled before college, backpacked through Europe that summer."

"Your parents let you do that when you were so young?"

"Let's just say I was a responsible eighteen-year-old, and at eighteen my mother and stepfather couldn't really stop me. I needed to get away and that was the way I chose to do it."

"I bet they worried about you the whole time you were gone."

"My mother was busy managing my father's company. Her marriage to my stepfather was still fairly new. I didn't feel they'd miss me."

"But they did."

"I could tell my mother did by the way her face lit up and she hugged me when I got home. What about your parents? Do they live in Thunder Canyon?"

This was territory where she didn't want to go, but she took a few footsteps in. "My mother does. She's an elementary school teacher. But my father left when I was five and we never saw him again."

"I'm sorry," Dillon said sincerely. "I know how hard it is to lose a parent, no matter how that happens."

She wanted to touch him now, the same way he had touched her. She longed to slip her fingers through the wave of hair on his forehead, or touch the line of his jaw that seemed so strong and determined. But she knew she should do neither. She knew she should back away.

She actually did take a step back. "I have to start my workout so I can get to the office on time."

"I won't keep you, then. I'll see you later."

"Later," she agreed, then headed for the StairMaster. She needed more than a sedate yoga routine today. She needed to expend some real energy. That way she could forget how Dillon's thumb had felt on her cheek. She could forget the way his body turned her on. She could forget the way she'd felt when he'd held her in his arms.

Late that afternoon, Erika studied the firmed-up details for Frontier Days. She found she accomplished more when Dillon *wasn't* in his office. His presence distracted her no matter how she tried to focus. That was unusual. She was usually good at focusing.

She heard the light footsteps in the hall and looked up when Stacy Gillette strolled in.

Dillon's "friend"—that's how Erika thought of her— stopped at her desk. "Is Dillon in?"

"Not right now. He's in a meeting upstairs. Would you like me to page him?"

Stacy didn't seem perturbed. "No. I'll see him soon enough."

A dinner date tonight?

As Stacy left the reception area, Erika told herself once more she shouldn't care what Stacy and Dillon meant to each other. But she did.

Time to focus again.

Turning to the computer, she printed out the schedule of events for Frontier Days. She was lifting the last page from the machine when she heard Dillon's bootfalls and took a deep breath as he strode in. Right away she noticed the grim expression on his face. His gaze met hers when he stopped by her desk.

"Is something wrong?" She didn't know why her voice wobbled a little but it did.

"We have a big problem. I had a meeting with Jeff's father. I can't talk him out of suing the resort. The whole situation is a mess. He's already called his lawyer and the resort is going to have to do the same. I have a meeting with Grant tomorrow morning. He's not going to be happy about this."

"Will the resort really be in trouble?" She could be out of a job in a minute if it was.

"Legal fees add up. Guest numbers are down. The resort still has its main expenses. Grant might have to think about cutting guest perks."

Erika suddenly heard noise in the hall—adult feet, the patter of *little* feet. Dillon turned toward the doorway just as Erika's mother and daughter entered in a burst of activity. That activity was Emilia. She was doing a combination of hopping and running in place.

As soon as she saw Erika, she pulled away from her grandmother and practically flew to Erika calling, "Mommee! Mommee!"

Erika opened her arms as her daughter launched herself at her. She felt the joy she always felt when she held Emilia close to her heart. After a few moments of mother-daughter bonding, Erika peered over her daughter's head at Dillon. His face showed surprise and then dawning understanding.

She *had* to say something. "Dillon, this is my mother, Constance Rodriguez, and my daughter, Emilia."

Dillon first shook her mother's hand. "It's good to

meet you." Then he turned to Emilia, a bittersweet expression on his face. "Hi, there."

Emilia turned into Erika's shoulder shyly but peeked up at Dillon.

"Say hello, baby," Erika encouraged her daughter.

Emilia opened one eye, rubbed her nose in Erika's shoulder, then grinned at Dillon.

"I can tell you're going to be a heartbreaker," he said. "Are you around two years old?"

"Soon," Erika offered. "In a few weeks."

Constance crossed to Erika and her granddaughter protectively. "I hope we didn't interrupt anything important. But I had a half day today and decided to pick up Emilia so we could have some quality time together. And speaking of time," she said to Erika, "when will you be home?" She addressed Dillon. "Erika puts in such long hours. I hope someone appreciates it."

"Mom!" Erika was embarrassed by her mother's comment.

Dillon stepped in. "I think her hours are long because she's taken on two jobs—being my receptionist as well as the coordinator for Frontier Days. I try not to keep her past five but I've noticed she tends to stay later."

"You leave at five?" Erika's mother asked.

"Usually. Unless I have a patient. But I'm on call in the evenings although I'm not in the office."

"Do you live here?" her mother inquired and Erika wanted to crawl under the desk. She tried again in a warning tone, "Mom…"

Dillon glanced from mother to daughter. "I live in a suite upstairs. That seems to be the best way to keep me available to the guests."

"I see." Her mother was obviously absorbing it all.

Had she stopped in today to meet Dillon because Erika had gone to dinner with him?

Emilia squiggled to be let down. Erika didn't want to let her daughter run free but there was little she could get into in the waiting area except magazines on the coffee table.

As Dillon watched the toddler, he commented to Constance, "Erika didn't mention she had a daughter."

"My daughter likes to keep her personal life to herself," Constance answered.

Erika noticed Dillon's gaze pass over her desk where no pictures or any personal effects were displayed and she could see the questions in his eyes, along with dark shadows she didn't understand. But she couldn't answer his questions here and now and didn't even know if she wanted to. He'd probably run in the other direction if he knew her history. He was so polished, so confident, so sure of his place in life. In so many ways he reminded her of Scott. Yet when she was alone with him…

Her gaze collided with his. Everything seemed to go quiet except for the beating of her heart.

Suddenly Emilia tired of pushing magazines on the coffee table. She ran for Erika but at the last minute detoured and headed for Dillon instead. She ran into his leg and he caught her so she wouldn't fall.

The toddler looked up at him and giggled as if what she'd done was great fun.

Erika stooped and caught Emilia again, lifting her high in the air. Emilia raised her arms and waved them. "Mommee, Mommee. Fwy!"

Erika explained, "She likes when I lift her up high so she can pretend she's flying." Instead of giving her daughter her way, Erika shook her head. "Not here. We'll fly at home."

The phone on Dillon's belt chimed. "Excuse me," he said, watching Erika with Emilia. He glanced at the caller ID. "I have to take this." He spoke into the phone. "Just a minute, Grant." Turning to Erika's mother, he smiled. "It was good to meet you, Mrs. Rodriguez."

"It was good to meet you, too, Dr. Traub."

Then Dillon came very close to Erika and gently ran his hand over Emilia's hair. "It was a pleasure meeting you, too, little one." His gaze was so tender yet filled with a deep emotion Erika couldn't read.

"I'll see you in the morning," he said to Erika. "Go ahead and leave. You were here early and put in a long day. Ruthann can handle any calls coming in now."

With a last wave for Emilia, he disappeared down the hall and into his office.

"You like him," her mother whispered to her. "That's dangerous."

"Don't worry, Mom. I learned my lesson the last time."

"I hope so." Her mother still looked worried.

Erika knew liking Dillon Traub was not going anywhere. She had even more to lose now than she had three years ago. She would not let a man ruin her life again.

At D.J.'s Rib Shack that evening, Stacy tilted her head and asked Dillon, "How often can you get away from the lodge?"

They'd been catching up over a dinner of ribs and corn bread. "I'm not chained here," he joked. "But I *was* hired to treat the guests so I don't like to go too far. If I do want to go out for an evening, I can give Dr. Babchek a call. He's retired and can back me up if Ruthann needs him."

The restaurant wasn't far from the main lodge. The

Rib Shack was nestled in among boutiques that stretched from the lodge through the resort.

Dillon glanced at the mural on the wall of the restaurant, the one D.J.'s wife, Allaire, had painted. For some reason, thinking about D.J. and Allaire and their two-year-old turned Dillon's thoughts to Erika and Emilia. The little girl was a miniature replica of her mother, glossy wavy hair, big dark eyes. She was a beautiful child—and Erika was a beautiful woman. Dillon sensed there was a lot more to his receptionist than met the eye. She seemed mature beyond her years, unless he was just trying to fool himself.

"Dillon?" he heard Stacy say.

"Yes."

"I asked if you've seen D.J. and Allaire since you've been back this time."

"Not yet. But soon, I hope."

"What were you thinking about?" the perceptive social director asked. "You seemed miles away."

"Not so many miles." Studying Stacy, he said, "I was thinking about my receptionist, Erika Rodriguez. Before I left the office tonight, her mother came in with her little girl. I didn't know she had a child and I wondered why she kept her a secret."

"Emilia's not a secret," Stacy muttered.

It was the way Stacy said it that made Dillon take notice. "Is there a hidden meaning there?"

Stacy hesitated and Dillon suspected why. She wasn't the type of woman who liked to gossip, but he wanted to know more about Erika and he wasn't sure she'd tell him herself. "I don't want you to reveal anything you shouldn't," he assured her.

"Can I ask why you want to know?"

Should he say that he was interested in her, when he

was trying to deny that fact himself? "We'll be working together this month. I'd feel better knowing something about her background."

Toying with a morsel of corn bread still on her plate, Stacy finally shrugged. "I suppose it won't hurt to tell you. Most of Thunder Canyon knows her story."

"Her story?"

"Oh, Dillon, you know how gossip spreads in small towns, especially here in Thunder Canyon. I'm sure tomorrow at the resort several people will ask me about *my* dinner with *you*."

"You're kidding."

She shook her head. "Think about the feud between Dax and D.J. and how that was all over town for years, especially after Dax and Allaire got a divorce and then D.J. started seeing her."

"Water under the bridge," Dillon muttered, knowing both of his cousins were extremely happy now. They'd settled their feud and actually become brothers. Not only that, but each had found the right woman to make them happy.

"Yeah, but that water has a lot of debris in it." Stacy pushed back her plate and propped her chin on her hand. "Erika was run through the gossip mill from one end of town to the other. After high school she waitressed for a while and took a couple of business classes in Bozeman. She'd settled into a job as a receptionist for a real-estate agency in Thunder Canyon when the boom took off. I think she intended to get her real-estate license eventually and start moving up. Then a businessman named Scott Spencerman came to town. He found a condo through Erika's agency, one here at the resort. Erika was only twenty-three. He was older, but she caught his eye. He flattered her and charmed her, gave her presents, but didn't particularly take her out in public much, if you know what I mean."

"No, I don't know what you mean. If he cared about her—"

"*She* cared about *him*. She thought she was in love with him. He was a businessman who traveled a lot and only wanted the condo here for skiing in the winter, and maybe some hiking in the summer. He didn't want a life here. He wanted entertainment while he was here."

"Stacy—"

"You asked," she drawled.

After a long pause, he asked, "So what was the gossip about?" He felt annoyed that people couldn't keep their noses where they belonged.

"The rumor was that Erika was a gold digger who took up with Spencerman for what he could give her."

"Is he still around?"

"God, no. When Erika found herself pregnant, he sublet his condo and disappeared. I don't know what really happened. I don't know if anyone does. But Erika was out of work after Emilia was born and I think things got pretty rough. Now she barely talks to anyone while she works and leads a very private life. No one really knows if the rumors about her were true or not. Many people thought she got what she deserved."

"A child and heartache?" Dillon asked. "Just what kind of people live here?" Dillon had met women who wanted to date him because of what he had rather than who he was. Erika didn't seem like that type at all. Could a whole town be wrong?

He thought about his mother and stepfather. Could a whole *family* be wrong?

"Are you interested in Erika?" Stacy asked, surprised.

He supposed that was because she knew he hadn't dated since he and Megan divorced.

"Will you tell me she's after my money if I say I am?"

"No. But I'll tell you to watch your back and your heart." She reached across the table and clasped his hand. "I know what you've been through—losing Toby and then your divorce. We're friends, Dillon. We have been since we were kids. I don't want to see you get hurt."

He smiled and shrugged off her concern. "How can I possibly get hurt? I'm only going to be here a month and then I'll be returning to Texas."

"A lot can happen in a month," Stacy prophesied.

Part of him hoped her prediction was wrong. The other part of him hoped she was right. He felt as if he'd been living in a bunker since Toby died…since Megan had left. In his group practice with three other doctors, he'd seen patients and dealt with insurance companies until he was too tired to see straight. Each night he'd gone home and collapsed, many nights falling asleep on the couch with the television blaring so it overrode his thoughts. Perhaps a casual relationship was the antidote he so desperately needed.

Erika has a child, he reminded himself.

Maybe Corey was right and it was time for him to leave his bunker…to bury his regrets and the guilt that he'd failed to save his son. He remembered again the way he'd felt at the Hitching Post with Erika in his arms. Would she say yes if he asked her out again?

He might just have to take a chance and find out.

Chapter Three

Dillon slowed on Thursday morning when he spotted Erika at the coffee bar not far from the main lobby. Usually he brewed a pot of coffee in his suite. This morning, however, he'd needed to go to his office, get to work…and forget.

He'd been awake most of the night, remembering the day his wife had left. She'd said, "Toby's gone and there's nothing holding us together anymore. I want a new life. I don't want to be married to a doctor."

He could have told her he'd leave medicine. He could have told her he'd work in management at Traub Industries and build the portfolio he'd inherited. In the end, he'd known if she couldn't accept his need to *be* a doctor, their marriage had truly collapsed.

With the old memories still ricocheting in his head and Erika standing about ten feet away, he decided he might need a *double* espresso this morning.

When Erika turned from the cashier, a tall coffee in her hand, he noticed the navy suit she wore projecting professionalism and decorum. It was a different style than the one she'd worn yesterday, with larger lapels… more fitted at her waist. Her very slim waist. The white silk blouse had a V-neckline. It was quite sedate, but the sedateness itself was alluring. She'd pulled her hair back from her face and secured it in a tight chignon, but there again the severity of the style just showed off the beauty of her face and her dark eyes.

Dillon checked his watch. When his gaze met hers, he motioned to one of the small, black wrought-iron tables. "I'll get my coffee and join you." He really didn't want to give her a chance to say no.

Indecision flickered across her face, but then she nodded and crossed to one of the tables, one a bit removed from the others in a shadowed corner. Did she not want anyone to see them together? Because of all that gossip Stacy had mentioned?

When he joined her, she was seated, staring into her coffee as if it held the schedule for her day. He didn't sit across from her, but rather beside her. She didn't move her chair away.

As she looked up at him, he asked, "So do you drink straight coffee or one of those exotic drinks?"

That's obviously not what she'd expected him to ask. "Do you really want to know?"

His arm was on the table and he leaned a little closer to her. "Yes, I want to know…in case I pick up coffee for the two of us some morning."

"I think that's on *my* roster of duties."

He shrugged. "Not necessarily. It's simply a courtesy. So what do you drink?"

"A double-shot latte. And you?"

"Straight espresso."

"Now that that's settled, why did you really ask me to join you for coffee?" she asked him, choosing to be direct.

"Because I like you."

Again, surprise showed on her face. "You always say the unexpected."

"Maybe that's because you think men are predictable."

Tilting her head, she studied him more assessingly. "So you're telling me you're not like most men."

"I don't know. What do you expect from most men?"

"That's beside the point." She lowered her gaze to her coffee again as if she didn't want to reveal any secrets.

Even sitting next to her like this, he could feel the attraction between them. He wouldn't let her put him in the same category as other men in her life. "That's *exactly* the point. You never told me why you ran away from me at the Hitching Post."

"I didn't run away," she protested, her chin lifting, her eyes flashing a bit, revealing passion he realized he'd like to tap.

He liked her flash. "You just evaded my question. Evading is pretty much the same as running away." If he challenged her, he might get to the root of the problem.

Her grip tightened on her coffee. "All right. It was the way you talked about possibly spending time with your cousins' children. You were so detached...like you were saying the words but you didn't really mean them."

She was perceptive...way *too* perceptive. After practicing the past few years, he thought he had his neutral face down pat. But this wasn't the place to tell her why he tried to be detached. To tell her about Toby…and Megan. "How did you interpret the detachment?"

She weighed his question, apparently understanding he was giving nothing away. "It meant you don't want the responsibility of children because you believe they're a burden. You don't necessarily 'like' kids."

"I like kids," he said quietly.

"And parenthood is a huge responsibility."

He certainly didn't disagree with her on that. But he wanted to keep this conversation about *her.* "Do you believe most men don't want the responsibility of fatherhood?"

After a few heartbeats, she finally replied, "I know two in particular who didn't—my father and Emilia's father. I'm sure you've heard gossip."

"Actually, I haven't. I had no idea you had a daughter. Why do you keep her a secret?"

"She's not a secret. Almost everyone in Thunder Canyon knows about her. But I try to separate my professional life from my personal life. I haven't always done that and I found it's better this way."

"No pictures on your desk? No mention of her?"

Erika set her cup on the table and her hand fluttered toward him. "I don't need a picture of her to hold her in my heart twenty-four hours a day."

"So essentially, you were just keeping her a secret from *me.*"

"Dillon, she's not a secret. I just—"

"You just didn't trust me enough to tell me about her. You didn't trust me enough to believe I'd understand what had happened."

Her gaze didn't evade his. "It's not as if we know each other."

Although he was physically attracted to Erika, there were so many other qualities he liked about her, too. Her blunt honesty was one of them. So he was just as bluntly honest. "Do you *want* to get to know me?"

It wasn't difficult for Dillon to see the turmoil Erika was in and he guessed one of the reasons why. "This isn't a boss-secretary situation, you know. You're a free agent. You're coordinating Frontier Days. You're just helping me out with my schedule and phone calls while I'm here."

Her brown eyes conveyed her concern. "You can still turn in a report about me after you leave that can affect my future."

Keeping his gaze on hers, he assured her, "I could write that report now and be done with it. It took me about an hour on our first day together to learn you're organized, you practically have a photographic memory and you're a perfectionist. What more could any employer want?"

"So you'd write a letter of recommendation now and file it away until you leave?"

"Yes. If doing that would mean you'll have dinner again with me tonight."

"I can't."

Dillon kept his expression neutral, denying how disappointed he felt. Maybe he was all wrong about the two of them connecting. Maybe he was the only one aware of the electricity in the air when they were sitting close together like this. But then he leaned back in his chair, leveled his gaze on her and knew he wasn't wrong. Still, this was her call. He wasn't going to pressure her.

"Okay," he said, pushing his chair back. "That's settled then."

But before he could pick up his cup of coffee, her

hand clasped his forearm. The electricity was there all right—sparking, buzzing, tingling.

"I have a commitment tonight," she explained. "It's a potluck dinner with some of the women in my neighborhood. But…" She gave him an intriguing half smile.

"But?" he asked, denying the fact his heart rate had sped up.

"But you're welcome to come along."

"Won't I be the only guy?"

"Is that too much of a challenge?" she teased.

He knew she wasn't teasing entirely. It didn't take a genius to realize this was probably some kind of test. She was throwing down a gauntlet. He'd spent much of his life picking up gauntlets. The future was always more exciting when he did.

"A potluck dinner sounds great. What can I bring?"

That evening Dillon's rented luxury sedan followed Erika's small Ford to an older section of Thunder Canyon, possibly an original section. The row houses—a mixture of brick, clapboard and stone—jutted in and out along tree-lined streets.

Erika pulled up in front of a narrow redbrick house that rose two stories. A windowsill box of colorful mums decorated the front window. The house next door, in gray brick instead of red, had a similar box at its front window.

As Erika stepped out of her car, Dillon joined her. She said, "I have to pop inside my place first to get my contribution to the supper, then we'll go over and gather up Emilia."

"Your mom lives next door?"

"Yes. It's more than convenient. It's wonderful really.

For a while I lived there with her and she wanted me to stay. But I needed a place of my own. This one went up for sale right when I was thinking of buying a house. I knew it was fate. It took every penny of my savings for a down payment, but I wanted something I could invest in and have for a lifetime, maybe even leave to Emilia someday. It's not very big, but it's perfect for the two of us."

She walked up the two front steps and unlocked the door.

Leaning against the wrought-iron railing, Dillon asked, "Mind if I come inside?"

"Not at all."

When Dillon walked in, he wasn't sure what to expect. But right away he could see this little gem of a house was something special.

She saw him looking down at the gleaming wood floors and said, "They just needed to be refinished. I did it myself with a little help from our neighbor."

"You do home improvement?" he asked with a smile.

"I watch the Home and Garden channel when I have a chance. I've learned a lot. I also go to the local hardware store and the clerks there fill me in on what I don't know."

The living room was to the right, off the small foyer. A braided rug in blue and green and yellow was surrounded by a comfortable-looking sofa and an easy chair in the same colors. Green throw pillows fringed in yellow picked up the colors in the curtains. An entire wall was devoted to framed photos of Emilia. Dillon felt the familiar lance to his heart as he remembered the photographs of Toby that had decorated his and Megan's living room.

Shaking off the shadows, he noticed a red washbasket full of toys that sat in one corner accompanied by a milk crate that held books. Passing the stairway to the second floor, they headed through the dining room into the kitchen.

"If you haven't guessed, I like blue and yellow a lot," she said with a wide smile.

Dillon glanced around the room at the yellow cupboards with blue accents, a round table with a high chair positioned at it and two shelves of cookbooks in a corner hutch. A circular, stained-glass window let in jewel-colored light even as the sun descended. The overall effect of the first floor was charming, and he could imagine Erika happily running after Emilia, bringing laughter into all of the rooms.

"What?" she asked him when she caught him staring at her.

"You're full of surprises. I never thought you'd dabble in paint or hardware."

"I'm a single mom, Dillon. I do what I have to do."

Yes, she was a single mom. He remembered being a dad. It sounded as if she'd always put her daughter first. He hadn't put his son first. Not until it was too late.

She unplugged the Crock-Pot on her counter. "We'll just put this in the backseat of the car. It will stay hot."

Dillon crossed to the kitchen counter to help her. Standing beside her, looking down on her, smelling that wonderful scent from her hair, he wanted to kiss her more badly than he wanted to do anything else. She was looking up at him as if she might want it, too. But he wouldn't rush anything with Erika. In fact, he shouldn't even think about starting anything with Erika. She had a child. They lived in two different states.

She has a child, he repeated to himself.

"I'll carry it," he said, his voice a bit husky.

"It's beef stew," she said. "Most of us try to stretch out paychecks so you'll see lots of casseroles, I'm afraid."

"There's nothing wrong with that."

She quirked up her brows. "Just how often do you eat casseroles?"

He finally had to admit, "Not often. But that's not because I don't like them. I just usually grab some take-out supper, or eat at a restaurant."

"No cooking skills?" she joked.

"No time to use cooking skills. That probably sounds like an excuse, but when I get home at nine o'clock some nights, the last thing I want to do is cook." With sudden insight, he said, "That's probably the same way you feel many nights, too, only you have a daughter to think about, so you don't have a choice."

Her eyes lingered on his. He thought her gaze dropped to his lips, stayed there a few seconds.

She brought her gaze to his again, then blushed a little. "Not many men understand that."

"Maybe the men you've known don't understand it, but I know men who do—Dax and D.J. particularly. Even *I* know that once children are in the picture, everything else should revolve around them."

They came a little closer to each other, toe-to-toe. If he set down the stew, it would be easy to wrap his arms around her and bring her in for a kiss. But he knew this wasn't the place or time to start something.

Still, he had the feeling something had *already* started.

"Speaking of children..." Erika joked, turning away to make sure everything was in order before they left. "If you put that in my car, I'll get Emilia. Sometimes it takes a little while to coax her into her coat. She can be stubborn."

Dillon went out the door first and Erika followed, locking the door. "I have a feeling you can be stubborn, too. Am I right?" he asked.

"Only when something is very important."

A few minutes later, Mrs. Rodriguez was peering out the door when Emilia toddled down the steps and ran straight to Dillon. He'd just finished settling the pot on the floor of the car next to a huge box of chocolates he was contributing to the supper and spun around at the sound of her laughter.

That sound tore at his heart. But he lifted her, unable to resist holding Erika's daughter. "Well, don't you look pretty in that red sweater."

She pulled a lock of her brown hair and grinned at him. "Cawwy…cawwy."

Erika came over to her daughter and lifted her from Dillon's arms. "I'll carry you."

But Emilia shook her head vigorously and pointed to Dillon.

Her gestures for some reason reminded him of Toby's. "Would you like me to put you in your car seat?" he asked the almost two-year-old, his voice strained, not knowing if she'd understand.

She reached toward him again. "Go…go…go."

Erika laughed and Dillon had to smile. At two, Toby had known what he'd wanted, too. When Dillon glanced at Mrs. Rodriguez, *she* wasn't smiling. She waved good-bye but didn't seem happy about her daughter driving off with a man. This Scott Spencerman must have done a number on them both.

A few minutes later, with Dillon driving her car, Erika was giving him directions to a church hall. It wasn't far and they didn't have time for conversation until right before they climbed out. Then she said, "Emilia doesn't usually take to men as she's taken to you."

"Why do you think that is?"

"She hasn't been around many men, so she sees them as strangers. But you— For some reason you're different."

Then Erika quickly unfastened her seat belt and exited the car.

Dillon watched as she expertly released Emilia from her car seat. But when Erika shut the back door of the car, Emilia reached her little hands toward Dillon. He could see Erika's look of surprise. He was surprised, too. And touched…in a deep but bittersweet way.

Erika started to explain to her daughter, "Dr. Dillon doesn't want—"

Dillon found himself responding impulsively, "Sure, Dr. Dillon will carry you inside. Come on."

Emilia was a little bundle of sweater and cotton overalls. She smelled sweet and he recognized the shampoo scent, the same brand Allaire used on her child. She laughed up at him, her sparkling brown eyes full of mischief. Then as suddenly as she'd reached for him, she tucked her little head under his chin and poked her thumb into her mouth.

"I think she could become attached," Erika said softly, a bit of worry in her tone.

"She's a real gift, isn't she?" he asked Erika, knowing what she'd been through.

"Yes, she is."

An elemental understanding passed between them. It was bone-rattling in a way. Understanding could be as potent as chemistry.

He wondered if Erika felt the understanding, too,

because suddenly she looked toward the social hall instead of looking at him, and said, "We'd better go inside." Then she went to the backseat for the Crock-Pot. After handing him the chocolates, they strolled up the walk, side by side.

Inside the social hall, Dillon was surrounded by the sound of women's voices. As he looked around, he realized this was indeed a test. Most of the women were accompanied by children. Already a few casseroles lined one of the tables. Paper dishes and plastic tableware marked each place. For once in his life, he wasn't exactly sure what he should say, or what he should do. He was bombarded by memories of Toby as he caught sight of children with their moms playing with toys, sitting at the tables.

Leaning close to Erika, he asked, "Will there be gossip about you bringing me here?"

"Not the way I'm going to introduce you. I thought you could give them some tips on nutrition and on keeping their kids healthy."

It was obvious Erika wasn't ready to go on a "date" with him. It was also obvious she was comfortable here—more comfortable than she was with her coworkers at the resort. "Okay," he agreed. "We'll ward off gossip with facts about nutrition. Why don't you introduce me? We'll start with that."

Erika clapped her hands for everyone's attention. The chatter ebbed away as the women looked at her expectantly.

"I want you to meet Dr. Dillon Traub. He handles emergencies and ailments at the resort. If you have any questions about the best foods to feed your kids, or how to keep them healthy this winter, feel free to ask him."

Dillon smiled at the women. "I don't pretend to know all the answers, but if I can tell you anything that will help, I'll be glad to do it."

Tired of being held, Emilia squiggled around in his arms. He raised his brows at Erika.

"You can put her down. She likes to roam from chair to chair. Mom already fed her because she usually gets caught up in play with someone here and doesn't eat."

After Dillon set Emilia gently on the floor and she ran toward another little girl who looked to be about three, he took off his suit coat and laid it across the table at the rear of the room. Then he tugged down his tie, slung it from around his neck and stuffed it into his jacket pocket. His shirt sleeves were next. He rolled those up and felt a lot more comfortable.

As he took a seat next to Erika, women began filling the chairs around the table, introducing themselves and asking him questions. They weren't shy and soon they were having a lively discussion about fresh foods, frozen vegetables and healthy snacks for kids. At one point, Dillon glanced at Erika and caught her watching him. Her interest gave him an odd feeling, but pleasurable and unsettling. What *was* he doing here? But then he realized, he enjoyed just being with Erika. The sound of her laughter entertained him, the curve of her hair against her cheek aroused him, her quick humor made him laugh. When her knee brushed his under the table, she quickly moved hers away. He felt sorry about that. The closeness of her body against his gave him an adrenaline rush he hadn't experienced in a very long time.

Scalloped potatoes, chili, black-bean soup and homemade bread were all very good and he complimented the chefs. These women knew how to stretch a dollar and do it well. From what he overheard, they seemed to rely on each other for babysitting and rides to work when their cars broke down. Here, Erika was among friends who supported her.

Erika was fielding Emilia's attempt to run around the table when Dillon caught sight of a young mother. She was holding the hand of a little boy who looked to be about five. As Dillon observed the child, he wondered if the boy had a fever. There was a glassy look to his eyes that Dillon didn't like at all.

The women were mostly finished eating and talking among themselves. He pushed his chair back and casually made his way to the young woman and her child.

When he crouched down by the little boy, he said, "Hi, there. What's your name?"

The little boy looked up at his mother.

"It's okay," she said.

"My name's Kevin."

Dillon extended his hand to the boy's mother. "Dr. Traub."

She took his hand hesitantly and shook it. "I'm Sue. Sue Kramer. Kevin isn't feeling well. He has a sore throat." Her arm went around her son's shoulders.

Dillon felt Kevin's forehead, then he took the boy's pulse. It only took a few seconds for him to be able to tell Kevin's heartbeat was fast. It was possible he could have strep, or it could simply be a virus. There was no way to know without a culture.

"I can't really do a proper examination here," Dillon said. "I'd like to make sure he doesn't have strep throat."

"Oh, but we don't have any insurance," she said, looking embarrassed.

"Do you have transportation?"

"Yes, my brother's pickup truck. Why?"

Erika came over to them then and asked curiously, "What's going on?"

"Kevin isn't feeling well," Dillon explained. "I'd like to take him to my office so I can examine him properly."

"Where's your office?" Sue asked.

"Thunder Canyon Resort."

"You're kidding! You want me to drive up there?"

Dillon could see she was uncomfortable with the idea.

"You really should get him checked out," Erika advised her. "If you're not comfortable going up there alone, I'll come with you. I really should drop off Emilia first then we can meet you there."

Sue looked from her son to Dillon, then at Erika. "I can't pay him," she said, her eyes becoming shiny.

Erika's gaze settled on Dillon.

He made a quick decision on how to handle this. "You made that black-bean soup, right?" he asked Sue.

She nodded.

"I thought it was great. How about if the next time you make it, you drop off a serving for me. The restaurants are great at the resort, but the truth is I get tired of restaurant food. Your soup would make a great lunch."

"You're serious? I mean I could easily make you some next week."

Dillon held out his hand to her. "It's a deal."

A smile came to Sue's lips and she shook his hand again. "Okay."

"We need about twenty minutes," Erika told her. "Then head up to the resort."

"I'll wait in my car until you get there," Sue told them, obviously not wanting to go inside by herself.

Dillon didn't try to convince her otherwise. "We'll meet you there," Dillon assured her, then he pushed Kevin's bangs across his forehead, remembering too vividly doing the same thing to Toby.

A little over an hour later, Dillon and Erika stood outside the side entrance to the main lobby of the Thunder Canyon Resort and watched the taillights of Sue's truck pull away.

"I'm glad it wasn't strep," Erika remarked as she watched the truck wind down the hill away from the resort.

"It will just have to run its course. But the vaporizer I gave her to use should help."

"Will the resort mind you giving that out?"

"She'll bring it back when she brings the soup. There are plenty more in the supply closet."

Erika turned to Dillon then, placing her hand on his arm. "That was a nice thing you did tonight."

"What? Acting like a doctor? She had a sick child. I had to do what I could for her…for Kevin."

The way Erika was looking at Dillon made him feel as if he'd accomplished some great feat. What she did next totally surprised him. Standing on tiptoe, she kissed his cheek.

Before he could stop himself, his arm went around her. She was slim but curvy and felt just right in his arms. She didn't pull away and he took that as a sign that she was as interested in him as he was in her. The light from the entranceway illuminated the area so he could see she was willing to stay just where she was. The wind lightly pulled a few strands of her hair from its mooring in her bun and they blew across her cheek. Her dark eyes sparkled.

"You're a beautiful woman."

"Thank you," she murmured, still looking up at him.

"I've wanted to kiss you since the first time I saw you."

"Dillon, we shouldn't even consider a kiss."

"*You* kissed *me*," he teased.

"That was just a thank-you kiss," she whispered.

"Maybe *this* could just be a thank-you kiss."

He really intended the kiss to be short and light and simple. But when his mouth settled on hers, when his heat ignited hers, it became more than a thank-you, more than short, much more than simple.

Her arms twined around his neck and he embraced her tighter. His mouth opened over hers and she responded in kind. She tasted so good, and she responded so passionately that his blood heated. He was more aroused than he'd been in years.

Then in a flashing instant, he felt the change. Her response came to a halt. He knew exactly what was going to happen. When he released his hold on Erika, she pulled out of his arms.

"I never should have done that," she murmured, her hand over her mouth. "I don't know what I was thinking."

"You weren't thinking, and neither was I."

She was shaking her head. "I can't get involved. I have Emilia to think of. I never should have kissed you."

He could see the panic in her eyes. The desire that had risen up in him when he'd taken her into his arms had rattled him, too. "Erika, it's okay. It was only a kiss."

"Only a kiss," she agreed, looking over his shoulder and a little less panicked. "I hope no one saw us," she murmured.

That made him frown. He wasn't ashamed of being with her. They hadn't done anything wrong.

But before he could put those thoughts into words, Erika stepped farther away. "I'll see you tomorrow."

The next moment she was running for her car, hopping inside, starting the engine. As she drove away, Dillon knew that taking advantage of her friendly kiss had been the *wrong* thing to do.

Chapter Four

All morning Erika had sat at her desk, answering the phone, printing guidelines for the stores downtown who were involved in Frontier Days. Still, she couldn't erase Dillon's kiss from her mind, or the feel of his lips on hers. Yet she had to try. She'd put so much time and effort and focus into getting her life back on track. She couldn't let a handsome doctor who was going to leave in a few weeks ruin everything she was building.

Still, she was curious about him. She wondered why, whenever Dillon was with children, she glimpsed so much sadness in his eyes. Would he ever tell her what that was about? Did she really *want* him to?

Entering the three-story main lobby of the resort from the corridor that led to the shops and restaurants, she noticed Dave Lindstrom standing by the life-size elk sculpture near the huge central fireplace. He was speaking with another guest. Crossing the vast lobby to reach the check-in desk, she was surprised when Dave's son Jeff approached her, casting a glance at his dad before he asked, "Can I talk to you? Maybe over there?" He pointed to one of the leather sofas that faced away from his father.

Crossing to the sofa and sitting down, Erika felt a sense of urgency about Jeff. She didn't know if she should talk to him with the threat of a lawsuit in the air, but his gaze was so beseeching she gave in. She had a few more minutes on her lunch break to spare.

She smiled at him reassuringly. "What would you like to talk about?"

He fidgeted with the hem of his T-shirt. "My dad said the chef who made my lunch got fired. And a lawsuit will cost the resort lots and lots of money and more people will get fired. Is that true?"

Jeff was mature for his age…and bright. The chef had in fact been fired, though she'd sworn she'd been very careful with his salad *and* his burger that day. Erika hesitated for a moment, then asked, "Why are you worried about this?"

"I watch the news. Dad has the cable channel on a lot. If people lose their jobs, they could lose their houses, too. And their kids won't have a place to live!"

He was upset and now she suspected why. Jeff was a good kid and what she saw in his eyes was…guilt. "Your dad said you had a salad and that's what caused your allergic reaction. If the chef *wasn't* careful…" She let her voice trail off, giving Jeff an opening to tell her what really happened.

Tears came to Jeff's eyes as he glanced toward his dad, then back at her.

She said gently, "Your dad loves you. All he cares about is that you're well again."

"He tells me over and over again not to eat anything someone else gives me. I have to eat stuff different from everyone else. It's no fun."

"I imagine it's not."

"I made a friend here. We went fishing together and skipped rocks and just walked."

"Who's your friend?"

"His name's Ken."

"Did you and Ken share something?" she guessed.

Jeff wiped his palms on his jeans. "He had this candy bar. He said it was just chocolate, no nuts. He gave me half of it and I stuck it in my pocket. That day at lunch when I saw that salad—" He sighed. "I just get so *tired* of salads. But Dad says they're good for me. He got a phone call and left the table and I just...I just ate that half of the chocolate bar. It wasn't supposed to have any nuts in it!"

Erika knew all that chocolate had to do was touch part of a conveyor belt where a nut product had lain. That was all it took for someone with food allergies to have a reaction.

She wasn't exactly sure what she was going to do with the information. She didn't want to put Jeff and his father at odds in a public place, or interfere in the proceedings if there was a lawsuit. So she simply asked, "It wouldn't be fair if your father sued the resort, would it?"

Jeff morosely shook his head.

"I do think it would probably be better if you told your dad instead of someone else telling him, though, don't you?"

"He's going to be so mad. I told you because..."

"Because you had to tell someone," she guessed. "What does your dad do when he gets mad?"

"He yells and his face turns a little red. But afterward he usually says he's sorry. He'll probably take away my computer privileges."

"You're a smart kid. I think you can find something else to do. I also think your dad will be proud of you for telling the truth."

"You think so?"

She'd seen firsthand the love that Dave Lindstrom felt for his son. She nodded. "I'm sure of it."

Opening her purse, she took a slip of paper from it. She wrote down her cell-phone number and handed it to Jeff. "If you get into too much trouble and you want somebody to talk to, just give me a call, okay?"

"I don't know when I'm gonna tell him."

"I know. I just want you to know you have a friend if you need one."

His father had finished his conversation and was walking toward them.

Erika asked Jeff, "Are you going to be okay?"

The boy nodded.

As Lindstrom beckoned his son to come with him, Jeff stuffed the paper she'd given him with her number into his pocket and crossed to his dad.

After a few minutes of considering her conversation with the boy, Erika decided what she was going to do. Following the hall back to the infirmary, she found Dillon in his office. He was filling in information on a patient's online chart.

His door was open but she rapped anyway.

When he looked up, he saw her, but his expression was unreadable as he said, "Come in." She realized he'd had a busy morning. Two guests had gone hiking and had fallen; another guest had expressed a problem with dizziness. Later, an older gentleman had rushed in with a nosebleed that wouldn't quit. Erika had already learned Dillon didn't let his chart work back up, and he e-mailed duplicate copies of the guests' infirmary visits to their family physicians. So he had a lot of info to enter.

"Did you have lunch?" she asked as an opener, not knowing where else to begin.

"Not yet. Ruthann just arrived. I'll take a break in a little while."

"I can pick you up something at the deli and bring it in."

"I told you before, Erika, that's not your job. You're not here to wait on me."

No, she wasn't. She was going to make a place for herself on this management team and become an asset to Thunder Canyon Resort.

"I was just in the lobby and Jeff Lindstrom asked to talk to me," she began, trying to keep her heart from tripping too fast.

"How is he?" Dillon's voice was full of obvious concern for the boy.

"He's fine. But feeling guilty."

"About?" Dillon stood and came around the desk to where she was standing.

"Employees getting fired because of him. He told me he'd made a friend. This friend had given him half a chocolate bar and assured him there weren't any nuts in it."

It was obvious Dillon was surprised. "He actually told you that?"

"Is it so difficult to believe an eight-year-old has a conscience and would confide in me?" she asked a bit defensively.

"No, of course not. I didn't mean it that way. Did he tell his father?"

She shook her head. "Mr. Lindstrom was in the lobby, too, and Jeff didn't seem ready. But he knows he has to now that he confided in me."

Dillon took another step closer to her. "Jeff coming to you was important. This cuts off the lawsuit at its knees...unless the boy denies the whole thing again."

"I don't think he will."

Dillon's golden-brown gaze was powerful as he suggested, "Denial is a great defense mechanism. We think it keeps us safe, but it really doesn't. The truth isn't far underneath."

She was intuitive enough to know Dillon wasn't talking about Jeff now. "Sometimes the truth can hurt, or put one in a dangerous situation."

"Dangerous? In some ways." He paused to study her. "I'm still thinking about that kiss. Are you?"

"Yes," she admitted on a sigh. Something about Dillon Traub demanded honesty.

"Do you feel if you became involved with me, you'd be putting your job in jeopardy?"

"I've thought about that...and other things."

"What other things?"

"I've been the butt of gossip before. I don't want to be again."

"That's one thing. What's another?"

"Emilia. Even if I were willing to take a risk for myself, I can't take risks with her."

"But there's still more, isn't there?"

"I don't have time to spare...not with Emilia and work and—"

"Okay, I get the idea. But I don't think I'm wrong about the attraction between us, am I?"

If she answered, she'd be putting too much power in his hands. She lowered her gaze, choosing not to let him see what was going on inside of her.

He lifted her chin with his thumb. "Erika?"

If she stood here much longer, she might end up in his arms! There was a magnetic pull toward him that could sweep her off her feet if she let it. But she had to keep both feet planted firmly on the ground. The touch of his finger on her skin, however, gave her thoughts wings. She couldn't seem to capture even one of them at the moment.

She had her purse slung over her shoulder and now her cell phone rang from inside of it. Saved by "Twinkle, Twinkle, Little Star"—Emilia loved to hear the song play on her phone—Erika dug in her purse. "I'd better get this." Opening the phone, she saw the caller ID and froze. It was Zane Gunther's manager! She couldn't believe it.

"Mr. Nolan! Hello. It's so good to hear from you." Even if it was bad news, at least she'd gotten this far.

"Miss Rodriguez?"

"Yes, it's me. I'm sorry. I was just so excited to receive your call."

The man had amusement in his voice when he asked, "So you think this is going to be good news?"

"I can hope, can't I?"

"Well, you must have been doing a lot of hoping since you first called me. I won't keep you in suspense any longer. Mr. Gunther has accepted your offer to appear at Frontier Days for the fee Mr. Clifton has offered to pay. He has one request, though."

She felt like jumping up and down for joy, spinning in a circle, grinning from now until next year. "Anything!"

"He would like a secluded place to stay before he performs."

She'd discussed this possibility, too, with Grant and had a couple of options. "We'd be pleased to give Mr. Gunther one of the penthouse suites, though that would be in the main lodge. A second choice would be for him to stay in one of the vacant condos. They're down the mountain a ways. A third option would be the most secluded. We have a few isolated cabins kept for dignitaries. They're off the beaten path and no one has to know he's there."

"That sounds perfect. Except…is the cabin large enough for anyone besides Zane?"

"The cabins are really more like small villas. Each has two bedrooms and a full kitchen as well as a dining and sitting area."

"I know Zane will want the cabin and I'll probably stay there with him. How about one of those vacant condos for the band?"

"Whatever you'd like, Mr. Nolan. I just can't believe you said *yes*."

He laughed, and said he'd be in touch again to finalize details. Then he ended the call.

After Erika hung up, she was beside herself with excitement. Zane Gunther. He was the *biggest* of all the stars she had tried to contact.

Dillon rose from his desk, his gaze questioning.

She couldn't keep her enthusiasm from what had just happened tied up inside her. "Guess who's coming to Thunder Canyon?"

Dillon's mouth tilted up in a smile. "The governor of Montana?"

"Even better. *Zane Gunther's* coming. Can you imagine? Think about the crowd he'll bring in! Just think about his music. And I get to sit in the front row."

"I'm glad you're happy about it. Convincing him to come could make Frontier Days an even bigger success."

"Aren't you excited? Don't you just love his music? Don't you wish you could shake his hand and—"

Something about Dillon's stillness alerted her that he already knew about this. She remembered telling him how frustrating it was not having anyone call her back… how much she needed a well-known country singer to perform…and he'd said he might be able to help.

Why would Zane Gunther come to Thunder Canyon? It wasn't a large venue like he was used to. Suddenly Erika knew this gig didn't happen by sheer luck. It didn't happen because *she'd* made a call.

"Did you know about this? Did you have something to do with getting him to accept my invitation?"

Dillon said simply, "Zane and I go way back. We went to school together."

"Oh, Dillon. Thank you." Before she thought about it once, let alone twice, she threw her arms around him and gave him a huge hug.

In response, Dillon's arms went around her.

Their enthusiastic embrace turned into something else when she raised her gaze to his. She could feel his muscles go taut under his suit coat. More than that, she felt his body heat, smelled his aftershave and fell into those golden-brown eyes. Whenever she was within touching distance of Dillon, her whole world changed. It became brighter, clearer, more adventurous. It was a no-holds-barred feeling that she could do anything, or be anything. It was so crazy, yet—

"Do you want another kiss as much as I do?" he asked, his voice husky.

"Yes," she breathed, waiting, anticipating, knowing she shouldn't be doing this but unable to help herself because it felt so right.

Dillon's mouth came down on hers quickly, possessively, passionately. His tongue breeched her lips, searched for a response which she willingly gave as he pressed her more tightly against him. As she laced her hands in his hair, the world around them fell away.

Eventually Dillon's hold lessened, his kiss slowed, his tongue stopped exploring and she was aware of all the changes. Yes, they both wanted this moment—but where did he think it was going to go? Where did she?

She dropped her hands from around his neck and backed away.

His voice seemed quite steady and he looked much less affected by the kiss than she was. "I shouldn't have done that here. Are you okay?"

His office was private. The scenery outside the long windows gave the illusion of being someplace other than in a lodge. But they were in the infirmary suite and could be interrupted at any time.

Erika's thoughts wafted through her mind. She was trembling so badly, she felt as if she wanted to fall to the floor in a puddle. But she couldn't let Dillon see how much he tilted her world.

After clearing her throat, she straightened her shoulders and met his gaze. "I'm fine."

The simmering heat in his eyes shook her all over again. He ran his hand through his hair and went to his desk, using it as a barrier between them. "You have an outside appointment this afternoon, don't you?"

With effort, she pulled herself together and replied,

"With Mayor Brookhurst. I'll be leaving in a few minutes. I have to sort through my notes first."

With an obvious effort to move the conversation away from the two of them, he remarked, "I suppose he'll be Master of Ceremonies for Frontier Days?"

"Yes. I want to go over his schedule. Bo Clifton and Arthur Swinton will be giving campaign speeches on Saturday afternoon of that weekend and probably glad-handing everyone they can. I'm hoping Mayor Brookhurst will look on the whole thing as one big retirement party."

Although they were discussing Frontier Days, Dillon was still standing there watching her. "What?" she asked.

"You're really beautiful when you let your guard down."

She wasn't sure what to say to that until Dillon went on. "You're beautiful *all* the time. But when you're enthusiastic, your eyes light up, and your smile is something to see. I'm glad Zane's concert will make you so happy."

She wanted to find out more about how this had all come about and exactly why he had asked his friend for this favor. "Did you have to twist his arm?"

"No," Dillon answered with a reminiscent smile. "I asked if he was free. He checked his schedule. I told him I'd be here this month and suggested we'd have time to reconnect. He seemed to like that idea."

"I'm hoping he'll enjoy himself here."

"This will be good for you in other ways, too. The prestige of having him and his band staying here could bring in even more guests. Grant will be thrilled. I guess your biggest job now will be to publicize it as quickly as possible."

If she kept looking at Dillon, kept thinking about his lips on hers, she'd end up in his arms again. So she concentrated on details. "There are so many things to think about—writing press releases, putting info on the resort Web site, taking out more ads across the area. I also need to know what Zane might need to be comfortable here. What does he like? What should I put in his room? Where can I get all of his CDs so we have enough to sell?"

"His manager won't mind you asking him those questions. He's a good guy."

"But *you* probably know his likes and dislikes, favorite candy bars. Unless he's into healthy snacks. If so, I need to know that," she said, still in awe that the country singer was actually going to perform in Thunder Canyon.

Dillon shrugged. "He's just a man, Erika, like any other. But if you need specifics, he likes corn chips and the hottest salsa you can find."

"Still—this is so big for Thunder Canyon."

"I'm getting a good idea of how big it is for you."

"Will you introduce us?" she asked impulsively.

"Sure. If I'm around when Zane comes in, I'll do that for you. You'll like him, Erika. He really is a regular guy."

"And you're a terrific…friend for doing this."

"I didn't do it just for you. Thunder Canyon can use a real economic pump. Maybe if other country stars see that Zane performed here, they'll follow."

"Thank you for any part you played in convincing Zane to come here. I promise, his experience is going to be a spectacular one. I'll make sure everything is exactly the way he wants it. We'll treat him as the celebrity he is."

"I think Zane will just want to have a beer and a rack of ribs from D.J.'s and act like a normal person. But that won't be possible if we get crowds. You'll have a chance to meet him outside the hoopla, then you can cross off one of your dreams come true."

One of her dreams come true. Did the other have to do with Dillon? She was so tempted by the idea. But she knew dreams faded away like smoke at the tip of a candle. She had to keep Emilia and her job first and foremost in her mind.

And if she and Dillon were drawn together again?

Silence stretched between them and Dillon looked sober for a moment. "I want to say this again. I know I shouldn't have kissed you here. I don't want to embarrass you or compromise you. But something seems to happen when we get within ten feet of each other."

He seemed as surprised by that as she was. She could pull back, wrap herself up in her professionalism, lift her chin and walk out without another word. But where would that get her? Dillon had said Zane was a real guy. Dillon was a real guy. He said what he meant. He did what he said. She wanted to be real, too.

"I learned in the past that an attraction can lead to pain I never want to experience again. Emilia deserves a family, not moments of happiness here and there. So I have to make a wise decision. Being attracted to you confuses me, I can't deny it. But right now I don't know what to do with it, either."

"So for now you want to pretend we're boss and employee and nothing else is going on."

"Yes," she admitted, relieved that he understood.

After all, she was a representative of Thunder Canyon Resort. She could not let desire for Dillon fog her better judgment.

And she couldn't fall into a month-long affair that would surely leave her with a broken heart. She couldn't.

"I have to go," she murmured as she broke eye contact and stepped toward the door.

"Good luck with the mayor," Dillon said, his voice wrapping around her as his arms had a few minutes before. She nodded and hurried out of his office, not knowing what to do about the tall, broad-shouldered Texan who had done her a huge favor.

Erika was walking through the main lobby of the resort when Erin Castro called to her from the front desk. Erin was still a mystery to many people in Thunder Canyon. She'd moved to town in July and found a job waitressing at the Hitching Post. Her long blond hair and very blue eyes, along with a figure straight out of Victoria's Secret, attracted men to her, especially when she'd been a waitress. But now she'd been hired at Thunder Canyon Resort on a temporary basis—to fill in where she was needed—and she wore more subdued makeup, often tying back her hair. Erika thought now Erin seemed to want to blend in with the crowd.

But she was still too pretty to just blend in. When Erika stopped at the desk, Erin asked, "How would you like to have lunch next week? We could get away from here and go to the Tottering Teapot."

"That would be nice." The bistro in town was a woman's haven.

Erika had made friends with Erin because she seemed so much less judgmental than other employees at the resort. Her other "lunch" friend, Holly Pritchett, was out of town for a few weeks. A relaxed lunch with Erin would help them to get to know each other better.

"The buzz around here is that you're doing a good job at putting together Frontier Days," she commented as if she was happy for Erika.

"Just wait until everyone knows," Erika said with a mysterious smile.

"Knows what? You act like you have a secret you can't wait to spill."

"It won't be a secret for long." She crooked her finger at Erin and they leaned close to each other. "Zane Gunther's going to be our entertainment."

Erin almost let out a whoop but stopped herself. "You're not kidding, are you?"

"Nope."

"I thought you looked excited about something. How long do I have to keep it to myself?"

"I'll be writing press releases tonight and sending them out to anyone I think can help publicize this. So by tomorrow evening, the news should be out."

"You look so happy I thought you'd have something good to tell me."

A guest, a woman who looked to be in her fifties, came in the front lobby door and wheeled her suitcase to the desk. Erin turned to her immediately.

Erika said in a low voice, "Call me to set up a lunch date."

As Erika left the lodge and headed for the parking lot, she wondered if the news about Zane Gunther had put the smile on her face...or if it had actually been the result of her kiss with Dillon.

The kiss with Dillon was winning—and that conclusion scared her.

Chapter Five

Later that afternoon, Erika returned to the infirmary as Dillon was seeing one of the guests to the door.

"Just keep that ankle taped for two days, Mrs. Bixby," he advised a gray-haired woman in her sixties. "Make another appointment to see me when you know your schedule. And use that cane."

The older woman smiled up at Dillon. "Maybe I can get one of those fancy canes with the flowers all over it. Or one with a nice wooden handle." She looked down at the utilitarian cane Dillon had apparently given her.

Dillon nodded. "I'm sure one of the shops will have them. But I think it might be best if you send your husband for one. You need to stay off of that foot, remember?"

"I remember," Mrs. Bixby grumbled as she hobbled out of the reception area into the hall.

Turning to Erika, Dillon gave her his full attention. "Was your meeting with the mayor successful?"

Just one look into Dillon's eyes and Erika knew he was thinking about their last kiss, just as she was.

"The mayor's easy to get along with," she answered lightly. "He agreed with everything I want to do."

Dillon laughed, then sobered as Mr. Lindstrom ambled into the reception area. Erika tensed, not knowing what was coming next.

After looking from Dillon to Erika, Lindstrom addressed her. "Jeff told me the truth a little while ago—about that chocolate bar. About your talk with him. Things *I* should have said to him. There will, of course, be no lawsuit. I should have explained better what could happen to him if his allergies got out of hand. But even *I* didn't want to think about that kind of reaction, let alone put fear into him."

Erika understood just how Mr. Lindstrom felt, the responsibility that weighed on him as a parent. Every day she had to make decisions about Emilia and she didn't know if they were right or wrong. "I think Jeff will be more careful himself now," she replied, knowing how guilty Lindstrom must feel.

"The two of you saved my boy's life, and I'd like to make up for the grief I caused you."

"You don't need to make up for anything, Mr. Lindstrom," Dillon assured him.

"Nevertheless, I want to. I don't know if you're aware of it or not, but I have a jet at my disposal," Mr. Lindstrom explained. "I thought maybe tomorrow the two of you would like to fly to Las Vegas for the day."

When Erika glanced at Dillon, she realized he was remaining silent because this was going to be *her* choice. She wasn't quite sure what to say. But then looking into her heart, she knew what she had to do, even though she'd never traveled outside of a hundred miles of Thunder Canyon. "Mr. Lindstrom, thank you so much for the offer. I appreciate it. But with my work schedule weekends are the only real time I get to spend with my little girl. I hope you understand. I'm sure if Dillon would like to get away—"

Dillon cut in. "I appreciate your offer also, but like Erika, I'm going to decline. I'm just settling in here and I think it would be better if I stick around."

Dave Lindstrom looked from one of them to the other. "I can see why I like the two of you. You both have a solid sense of responsibility. Well, if ever either of you need anything, just let me know." He offered them both business cards. "All my numbers are on there. If you ever need my assistance in any way, I'll be glad to help out. Jeff and I will be here until after Frontier Days.

"Well, I won't keep you any longer." He shook Dillon's hand and then Erika's. "I'll be seeing both of you around." With a grin and a wave, he left the infirmary.

"If I had said yes to the trip to Las Vegas, would you have gone?" Erika asked, knowing exactly what a trip like that with Dillon could lead to.

"I would have, if I could have gotten Dr. Babchek to cover."

Her voice was a little shaky as she asked, "And what would the two of us have done in Las Vegas?"

"We would have gone to a show, toured the city, eaten in one of the spectacular restaurants." Then he touched the side of her cheek with the back of his hand. "And we would have gotten to know each other a little better."

His touch made her insides tremble and she hated

feeling vulnerable to him. She hated the idea that he could get to her like this.

"And what would you have expected in return?"

Dillon tilted his head and studied her for so long she began to feel very uncomfortable. Finally, he said, "Erika, why do you expect the worst whenever you're with a man?"

"I don't expect the worst. I just expect to be let down."

"Then you haven't been associating with the right men," he replied with a lifted brow.

She felt her cheeks burn. Was she wrong to lump him in the same category as Scott?

He checked his watch. "I'm expecting a patient in ten minutes and I need to go over her chart."

For a moment Erika thought he was angry with her until he said, "For what it's worth, I admire your devotion to Emilia. Only a good mother would have made the choice you did."

Then he was walking away from her and she realized how much she wanted to be held in his arms.

"So tell me about Dr. Traub," Constance Rodriguez said as she sat at Erika's kitchen table after church on Sunday, watching her granddaughter pull a toy duck around the table. It quacked every once in a while, making Emilia giggle.

This conversation wasn't going to be an easy one to have, Erika realized as she stood at the stove and flipped an omelet. "What do you want to know?"

"Do you like working for him?"

"One of the reasons I accepted the position was to have weekends off. It was so wonderful to have yesterday and today with Emilia. A seven-day rotating schedule just didn't seem to give me as much time with her."

"I agree, having a weekend with her must seem like a wonderful gift. But I didn't ask if you liked the *schedule*."

Erika took her attention from the frying pan and looked at her mother. "I like him."

"*More* than like him?"

When she thought about their kisses, she felt her cheeks coloring. "I've only been working with him for a short time, Mom."

"Erika…"

She lowered the heat on the burner, trying to decide what she wanted to say.

"Okay, I *more* than like him. So don't say what you're thinking."

"How do you know what I'm thinking?" her mother asked ingenuously.

"I can imagine. I know the mess I've made of my life before. I won't do that again. I know Dillon is leaving in a few weeks. Still— He makes me feel as if I'm his equal. He's respectful of me and he…he…" She certainly couldn't tell her mother that Dillon was hot, absolutely smoking hot from his head to his toes. "And he's kind."

"That's *not* what you were going to say, Erika Rodriguez. I'm not too old to notice a good-looking man. I just don't want you to like him for the wrong reasons."

"What would those reasons be?"

Emilia ran around the table, the duck catching on one of the table legs. When she started to fuss, Erika crouched down, pointed to the string and showed her how to unwind her toy until it was free again.

"I understand he comes from money," her mother

said. "He's a doctor. He's older than you are. I can see how you would look to a man like that to...take care of you."

"Mom, how can you say that? For the past three years, all I've wanted to do is to live on my own, mother on my own, take care of Emilia on my own."

"And it's hard, isn't it?" Her mother's eyes searched for the truth.

"Yes, it's hard. But it's also satisfying. I'm working to build a future for two. That gives me motivation and a goal. My life isn't just about me anymore, it's about the two of us. I don't like Dillon because of everything you mentioned. I like him because—"

She took a breath and needed a moment to say something her mother could accept. After switching off the burner, she flipped the omelet on to a plate.

"Tell me," her mother prompted.

"If I tell you, you'll laugh."

"Try me."

"He makes me feel alive. He makes me feel like I'm more than I am."

Her mom didn't laugh, but now she looked really worried. "You've fallen for him. Erika, I don't want to see you get hurt again."

"I don't want to get hurt again, either, but I haven't dated in three years, Mom. I haven't wanted to be with a man for three years. Being near Dillon makes me want things again." She wasn't going to go into what those things were, but from the look on her mom's face, Erika could tell Constance got the gist.

This time as Emilia came around the corner of the table, her sneaker bumped a chair leg and she fell. Both Erika and her mom rushed to her.

"You're okay," Constance assured her granddaughter. "Come on, let me help you up."

As soon as she was standing again, Emilia toddled to her mom and wrapped her arms around her. Caught in the little girl's embrace, Erika gazed at her mother. "Don't worry about me, Mom, I'm going to be fine."

Constance laid one hand on her daughter's shoulder, and the other on her granddaughter's hair. "I don't know if you will be fine. But I trust you to know what's best for you."

Erika had been thinking and organizing and planning her future ever since the day she'd found out she was pregnant. She wouldn't stop now just because Dillon Traub's kisses turned her insides to mush.

All weekend, Erika had thought about how close she'd been to going to Vegas with Dillon. The idea of it gave her that going-over-the-top-of-the-Ferris-wheel feeling and she wasn't even sure why, given what a co-lossal mistake that would have been.

Yet as she locked her purse in her desk drawer Monday morning and switched on the computer, she knew she looked forward to seeing him in spite of every good reason to keep her distance. Because Dillon was as punctual as she was, Erika listened for the sound of his footsteps. She was sipping her cup of coffee when she heard them.

Something was different. His stride was usually quick and smooth with an athlete's agility. This morning, however, when he appeared beside her desk, she knew something was definitely wrong. There was a scrape on his jaw and his breathing was deliberate and slow.

"What happened to you?" she asked, knowing whatever had, it was none of her business.

A smile broke slowly across his lips. "I scored."

For a moment, his words didn't compute. Then she realized he'd been involved in some kind of sport.

"I don't suppose you were bowling?" she asked with a lifted brow.

He laughed and put a hand across his ribs. Shaking his head, he said, "Touch football."

"With enemies or friends?"

"Dax, Marlon Cates and a few others."

He took a deep breath and seemed to wish he hadn't. In fact, he'd even gone a little pale.

She hurried around the desk and stood very close to him. "Are you sure you're all right? Maybe you should call Dr. Babcheck and just go up to the suite and rest."

Now he looked a little angry. Straightening, he dropped his arm to his side as if to prove he was fine. "Just a few bruised ribs. I don't need to call my backup. I'll be in my office if anyone needs me."

Then as if he didn't want her asking any more questions or studying him further, he went down the hall to his office, his posture almost in a military stance as if he had to prove something to her.

As Erika answered the phone, fed information to reporters about Zane's concert, worked on schedules for activities for Frontier Days and made multiple lists for everything she still had to do, she found herself worrying about Dillon and wanting to check on him. Because he was her employer?

Hardly.

Because he'd kissed her?

It wasn't just that, either.

At lunchtime, she decided she really needed to look in on him. She could do that easily. She'd ask him if there was anything he wanted for lunch, even though he'd told her she didn't have to do that.

But when she stood before his closed door, knocking didn't seem easy after all. Gathering her courage, she did it anyway.

He called, "Come in," with less forcefulness than usual, she thought.

Dillon was seated at his desk, a medical journal open in front of him. She noticed some papers that had apparently floated off the printer and onto the floor. Automatically she went to them to pick them up.

"I can get those," he told her and stooped to do it. But when he did, she could see his grimace, the pain evident on his face with his quick intake of breath.

"Dillon," she said gently, crouching down beside him, scooping up the papers that had fallen there. "You shouldn't be here. In fact, I'm pretty sure you should be at the emergency room. You need to see a doctor."

"I *am* a doctor, Erika. Even if I cracked a rib, there's nothing I can do for it but let it heal."

He was one stubborn man, but that didn't surprise her. Males usually were stubborn. She dismissed the fact that *she* could be, too. "Just what would you tell a patient in your condition?" she challenged him.

"I'd tell a patient to rest," he grumbled, almost under his breath.

She clasped his forearm and when she did, the connection she felt to him was hot and tingling. "And maybe you'd advise them to take some pain medication?"

"I'm not taking pain medication," he snapped. "I'll tough this out today and I'll be fine tomorrow."

Exasperated with him, she stood. "I could call Ruthann and ask her to come in a little early."

"Her regular hours are fine. *I'm* fine."

"Sure you are, and I'm Miss U.S.A."

Now he cracked a grin. "You *could* be."

"That's not in my life plan."

He turned serious now. "Just what *is* your life plan, other than becoming a resort manager someday?"

"It's not complicated. I just want to be a good mother to Emilia and help her grow into an independent young woman."

"But what do you want for yourself?"

"I haven't had time to think about that."

"I think you've thought about it, but you were so hurt by your last relationship you've closed off the possibility of another one."

At his all-too-perceptive comment, Erika suddenly realized how badly she wanted to avoid this subject. For the past three years, she'd shut down desires and dreams. Dillon confused her and almost made her want to resurrect them again. But that risk was just too great.

Moving around his desk, she automatically picked up his empty coffee cup and tossed it into the waste can. "I'll be away from my desk for a little while. I'm meeting a friend in town for lunch, then taking care of last-minute ads with downtown businesses."

After a few silent beats, he said huskily, "You're evading again."

Turning on her heel to face him, she said, "I'm just evading for *now*."

"All right."

"I can bring you a sandwich from the deli before I leave."

"I'm not hungry. If I want something later, I'll go get it."

"You're acting like a macho male."

He gave a shrug. "What makes you think I'm not?

You're my receptionist, Erika, not my nurse. You're not getting paid to hover."

She knew the expression on her face gave away the hurt she felt at his words, and she knew what she had to do. Leave.

Turning away quickly so he couldn't see her expression, she said, "I'll buzz you when I'm back."

On her way out of his office, she thought he called her name.

She just kept walking.

After Erika returned from her appointments in town, the late afternoon turned busy. The phone rang, with one of the guests calling in to say she thought she had the stomach flu. Erika told her to come right down. While Dillon was examining her, another guest called. He'd sprained his ankle while golfing. A newly checked-in patron had wrenched her back while pulling her suitcase. And so it went. It was just one of those days and as Dillon came to the reception area after his last appointment, he looked pale. From his furrowed brow and the lines around his eyes, Erika could tell he was in pain. She hated seeing him like this. But he'd made clear that he didn't want her help.

Ruthann had arrived so Dillon didn't linger, just left the infirmary, telling Erika he'd see her tomorrow.

He should stay in bed tomorrow and let himself heal, she thought to herself. But Dillon obviously didn't want advice on what was good for him and what wasn't.

Erika's own work kept her tied to her computer for a while longer. Yet she couldn't take her mind off of Dillon—the way he'd looked when he left, how he'd hidden his symptoms from his patients all afternoon.

Since she was planning Frontier Days, she'd been

given a card key to take the elevator to the penthouse floor, in addition to all the other floors. Closer to the event, she'd be posting signs and erecting billboards advertising all aspects of the festival. The resort's aim wasn't only to attract tourists to Thunder Canyon and the lodge, but to encourage their guests to attend all the activities in town, supporting businesses there, encouraging guests to return the following year.

Erika thought about the card key. She could just go up to Dillon's suite and knock on his door. If he didn't answer, he was probably resting and she'd just leave again. Or maybe not. She might try to phone him from outside the suite just to make sure he was okay.

Her mother was used to her working late so a few more minutes wouldn't matter. Dillon's health was important to her, though she didn't examine all the reasons why too closely.

The plush carpeting in the hall muffled her footsteps as she approached his door. Wrought-iron sconces with their candlelight bulbs on the wall lit her way. Outside his door, she hesitated and knocked.

When she heard a muffled, "Just a minute," from inside, she was relieved.

He opened the door and looked astonished to see her. "Erika! I was expecting room service."

"Sorry, I'm empty-handed," she joked.

He was wearing a gray sweatshirt and sweatpants and didn't look much better than when he'd left downstairs. "Is something wrong? Did you need something?"

"I was worried about you," she blurted out. "You looked terrible when you left. The truth is you don't look much better right now."

"Oh, thanks. That's great for the ego." Amusement danced in his eyes, along with the pain he must be feeling. "Come on in. I really do need to sit down," he said with a loud exhale of breath.

He crossed to the living room and sank down onto the sofa.

She hurried to him and sat beside him. "You really should go to the emergency room, Dillon."

"Let's not go over this again. As soon as room service comes, I'll eat dinner, get a shower, ice my ribs and go to sleep for the night."

She should leave. She really should. But sitting next to him on the sofa like this, her arm lodged against his, her knee almost brushing his, she felt the urge to stay, even though she knew she couldn't.

"How long ago did you call room service?"

"Only about ten minutes. It could be a little while until they arrive if they're busy."

Their gazes connected…held. Erika could see Dillon's beard stubble. She wanted to smooth her hand over his jaw and comfort him in some way.

"Tell me about Scott Spencerman," he requested.

That was the last thing she'd expected him to say. "Why?"

"Because your experience with him affected your life and I'd like to understand."

"I don't talk about Scott. He's in my past."

"Is he? Or is he the reason you don't want to think about getting closer to me?"

Her heart ticked off a few vibrating seconds until she replied, "There are lots of reasons why I shouldn't get closer to you."

"I know. There are a lot of reasons why *I* shouldn't get close to *you,* too. But here we are. So tell me about him."

Sitting beside Dillon like this on his sofa felt intimate,

though Erika wasn't sure why. They were just sitting there talking, fully dressed, with no intention of doing anything else. Maybe it was the subject matter. Maybe it was Dillon's voice, gravelly and gentle and encouraging.

After taking in a deep breath, she blew it out and stared straight head. "I was young and naive," she murmured. "After high school, I waitressed, took a couple of business courses and finally ended up in that real-estate office. I was itchy for something else, not sure what I wanted, still living with my mother. I wasn't… I didn't…" She cast Dillon a sideways glance, intending to look away again. But his gaze locked to hers.

"I didn't sleep around," she finally said bluntly. "I dated, but not for sex. I was looking for somebody special. When I met the right person and we fell in love, then sex would mean something. Scott seemed to be everything I'd ever wanted. I wasn't experienced enough to understand he never intended to stay in Thunder Canyon. More importantly, he never intended to take me with him if he didn't. When he talked about Rome and Singapore and Cancun, I thought in the future we'd go there together as a couple…as a married couple. I didn't see the warning signs. He'd only see me on certain nights at certain times. I just figured he had calls to make and business to take care of. It wasn't until afterward I found out he was also dating someone in Bozeman. Everyone gossiped about me, but no one told me the truth."

Dillon took her hand in his. "Would you have wanted to see the truth? Would you have listened?"

No one had ever asked her that question. She gave it a long moment of thought. "Maybe not. But when I became pregnant and Scott told me he never wanted to get serious, that he wasn't just dating *me*, that he'd be leaving soon, I didn't see it coming. I was so foolish," she said shaking her head.

"You were young without much experience with men."

"I was stupid. But Emilia is the wonderful result. She's helped me grow up and I love her to pieces. Now I'm just grateful I have her and I try to forget the rest."

"How often do you hear from him?"

"Never. He's not in our lives. When he left, he made it clear he wanted nothing else to do with me, or a baby."

"He doesn't pay child support?"

"When I was out of work after Emilia's delivery, I considered trying to find him. But if he paid child support, I'm afraid he'd want something in return. If he doesn't care about his daughter, I don't want him anywhere near her. I'll raise her on my own."

"Does he know he has a daughter?"

"No. But if she wants to search for him one day, I'll help her. For now, it's just the two of us and that's okay. We've got a good life."

"I can't imagine a man wanting nothing to do with his child," Dillon murmured.

"That's because you're a different kind of man," Erika said, part of her knowing it, part of her afraid to believe it. That pained expression was back in Dillon's eyes... as if he didn't agree with her assessment. But he lifted their hands, studied their entwined fingers and leaned a little closer to her.

She lifted her chin, anticipating his kiss, ready to feel his arms around her again.

He enfolded her in his arms, began a heart-tripping kiss, but then pulled away. "You've had a raw deal once and I don't want that to happen again. In a few weeks, I'll be leaving. We both need to remember that."

The problem was she still wanted him to kiss her, even though she knew he'd be leaving. Was she willing to risk falling in love with Dillon Traub—and having her heart broken all over again if she did?

Chapter Six

Fifteen minutes later, Erika paced Dillon's living room. She'd agreed to stay until he was finished in the shower. What if the pain in his ribs suddenly got worse?

Dillon had left his cell phone on the occasional table next to the sofa. Just as she heard the shower turn off in the bathroom, his phone chimed. Crossing to it, she picked it up and saw Dr. Babchek's number in the caller ID.

Hurrying to Dillon's bedroom, she peeked inside the open door. Apparently Dillon was still in the bathroom. "Dr. Babchek's on your cell," she called. "Should I answer?"

The bathroom door opened a crack. "Yes. Thanks. I'll be out in two minutes."

She opened the phone and greeted the caller, just as she would if she were sitting outside Dillon's office. "Good evening, Dr. Babchek. This is Erika Rodriguez,

Dr. Traub's receptionist. Can you hold for about two minutes?"

"I can hold," Dr. Babchek told her in a deep voice that wasn't the least bit impatient.

Erika retreated to the hall outside of Dillon's bedroom. It didn't seem right to be inside.

When he finally emerged, her breath caught. His hair was still damp from his shower and looked tousled, as though he'd run a towel over it. He was wearing black jogging shorts but there were still beads of water in his chest hair and on his very muscled upper arms. He might as well have been naked the way her heart was racing.

When his gaze landed on her, she blushed and handed him the phone. Although she'd been overwhelmed by the virility emanating from Dillon, she'd still caught sight of the bruising on his left side, which looked bad even to her untrained eye.

She walked beside him into the living room as he said into his phone, "Ron. It's good to talk to you again. I wondered if you could cover for me tomorrow morning at the resort. I have an appointment at Thunder Canyon General Hospital."

The doctor must have answered him in the affirmative because Dillon stopped before heading into the living room and nodded. "That's great. I'll let Ruthann know you'll be there until noon."

When Dillon closed his phone, Erika couldn't help but ask, "Are you getting checked out at the hospital?"

He shook his head. "You worry too much. No, this is business. I have an appointment with the Chief of Staff."

She supposed it wasn't unusual for doctors to consult with each other and she had no right to delve into Dillon's business.

"If you didn't have to get home to Emilia, I'd ask you to have dinner with me tonight," he said casually.

Her gaze lingered on his eyes and then his lips and then his upper body. She swallowed hard. "I do have to get home."

When he set his hands on her shoulders, her stomach somersaulted. He asked, "Why did you come up to my suite tonight?"

She licked suddenly dry lips. "I told you I was worried about you."

Silence wound about them, intensifying pheromones, need and awareness. Whatever bond they were forming drew them closer together. Erika breathed in Dillon's freshly showered scent, longed to feel his skin against hers.

When Dillon wrapped his arms around her, she wound hers around his neck. His body was hard against hers. His mouth took its time with her as he nibbled at her upper lip and lined it with his tongue. She touched his upper lip with hers, thinking that would be the tinder that burst their kiss into flame. But he apparently had more self-control than she did because his lips trailed kisses across her cheek and down her neck. She moaned, feeling weightless in his arms.

Every thought skittered away into pure physical sensation. Then his hands were in her hair, his lips sealed to hers, and the taut pressure gave way to erotic invasion. His kiss seemed to go on forever. She responded to every thrust of his tongue, playing a game of tease and retreat. She felt the shudder that ran through his body and knew they were both dabbling with desire that could explode and hurt them both. Still she couldn't seem to get enough and neither could he. If his ribs were bothering him, desire must have overridden any discomfort he felt.

The kiss might have urged them to his couch. They might have ended up in his bedroom. But she'd never know because there was a knock at his door.

They both froze.

Dillon pulled away from her just a few inches, called, "Just a minute," and kept her in his embrace.

She had to find her composure and quickly. This had been a test and she'd failed it miserably. If that knock hadn't sounded on the door—

She backed away from Dillon...a good foot away. With a deep breath, she let her gaze trail down his upper body again, and it settled on his bruises. She brushed them lightly with the back of her hand, and he winced, obviously in greater pain than he was willing to admit. "While you're at the hospital tomorrow, please get this checked out."

She felt his hot gaze on her as she crossed to the table and picked up her purse. Then she went to the door and opened it, welcoming the waiter and Dillon's supper... escaping back to a life that was safe.

The following evening, Dillon walked up to Erika's house and pressed her doorbell. Today he had been suddenly aware of time ticking away. He was dissatisfied with allowing his career to become his life. Considering the past few years, he was downright fatigued by beating himself up about his failed marriage...about the god-complex he and other doctors had that they could cure a child in spite of the odds. He also realized he needed to remember Toby *well*—not sick—and the good times they'd experienced, rather than all the moments he'd missed.

He'd spent the morning at the hospital, thinking about his future, discussing options with the Chief of Staff who understood the needs of Thunder Canyon residents. By the time he'd returned to his office, Erika had gone for the afternoon, working to finalize events for Frontier Days. He'd missed her. He didn't know what this feeling of connection to her was, but he needed to pursue it.

So here he was, standing at her front door, rationalizing why he'd come, why he was carrying a present for her daughter.

Before he'd left the resort, he'd been steeped in decisions about what came after September. Should he accept the offer to join the concierge practice in Texas? Should he stay near his family? Should he make a move and maybe find a new life in Montana? He was grateful he had choices, but the choice right now didn't seem clear. This evening, getting away from the resort and his suite had just seemed like a good idea.

The chime from Erika's doorbell echoed inside. He felt a rush of adrenaline when she answered the door wearing a thigh-length red sweater and black leggings. Her mass of loose waves tumbled around her shoulders and all Dillon wanted to do was run his fingers through them.

Her brown eyes were huge with questions. "This is a surprise."

Her gaze ran over his black sweater and khakis, and he liked the fact that she looked at him the way he looked at her. "I should have called."

"But you didn't."

She was the kind of woman who wouldn't let him get away with anything. "If I had called, you could have easily given me an excuse not to see me. Are you busy?"

As if on cue, Emilia's voice came from inside. "Mommy, pway."

"I'm a mom," she reminded him. "I'm always busy.

But I've fed Emilia supper and this is our winding-down time. Come on in. How are your ribs?"

"They're better. Nothing is broken." He'd had them x-rayed while he was at the hospital.

"Did you have supper?"

"Yes. Sue dropped off some of her soup and home-made bread."

"She's a good cook."

Whereas Erika's living room had been straightened up the last time he was here, now it had a different look because it had been a two-year-old's play area for the past couple of hours. Sofa cushions stood cockeyed against the furniture with a blanket draped over the top. Stuffed animals, dolls and doll clothes lay scattered across the rug. Children's books covered the top of the coffee table, while a coloring book and crayons were left abandoned on the easy chair. The whole atmosphere gave his heart a pang that was warning him he'd made a mistake by coming.

Erika scooped up a few toys and cut him a sideways glance. "Be careful not to trip over anything."

Emilia was on her hands and knees peeking out of her hideaway at him.

"Hi, there," he said, crouching down. "Remember me?"

She grinned and crawled out a little farther. "Doctor, doctor."

"She remembers," he murmured, stunned by the wonderful-terrible recall of a child. Toby had been like that, too—quick to remember, quick to make friends.

"She remembers what she wants to remember, so you must have made an impression," Erika joked.

"That could be good or bad," he said drily. "Come

here, Emilia, I have something for you." He wiggled
the box.

Emilia scrambled out from under the cushions and
blanket, pushed herself to her feet and ran over to him.
One of her little overall straps was falling over her shoulder. She bumped against Dillon's knees, holding on to
them to balance herself.

He pushed her shoulder strap up where it belonged
on top of the little white blouse covered with dancing
dogs. "Would you like to open this?"

He set the box on the floor because it was too big for
her to handle. Emilia squatted down beside it.

Erika said, "What do you say, baby?"

"Tank you," Emilia told Dillon with a little smile.

"You're very welcome. I hope you like it."

Dillon helped Emilia with the package, which pic-
tured a busy box with lights and music on the box.

"I already put the batteries in," he told Erika.

"You've thought of everything." Her eyes were full
of questions, questions he didn't know if he could answer.

After Dillon helped Emilia open the box and extract
the toy, he pressed one of the buttons. A tiger popped
up, music played and a blue light flashed.

"Oh, she's going to love this," Erika murmured.
"Lights and music fascinate her right now." She dropped
to the floor beside her daughter and sat cross-legged,
grinning as Emilia pushed the next button and an elephant popped up with a green light flashing.

Emilia giggled. Pointing to the elephant, she said,
"Dumbo."

"That's the elephant in one of her books," Erika explained, with a mother's pride that her daughter was
learning.

As Dillon watched mother and daughter, as he joined in laughing with them, seeing Emilia learn, his heart burned with remembered warmth. The feeling was bittersweet. Pictures of hugging Toby, reading to him and kissing him good-night played across a screen in his mind. Then it was swiftly followed by a feeling of powerlessness because he hadn't been able to keep his son from slipping away.

Suddenly Emilia stopped playing with the toy. She climbed to her feet, ran to Dillon and held her little arms up to him. "Huggy, huggy," she said as if he should know what that meant.

Dillon sought Erika's gaze for translation.

"She wants a hug, and she wants to hug you."

With a lump in his throat, Dillon wrapped his arms around Emilia and, ignoring the pain in his side, lifted her onto his lap. He gave her a hug and she hugged him back, burying her face in his sweater.

He ran his hand over her wavy hair, feeling his throat tighten.

"I think she's getting sleepy." Erika's voice was low and husky and he wondered what she was thinking. But she didn't tell him as she gathered Emilia from his arms. "Come on, honey."

But Emilia began fussing and pointing to the toy Dillon had given her.

"All right. We can take it to your room. But you can't have it in bed with you."

"I'll bring it," Dillon said.

Erika's gaze sought his. "This could take a little while. Sometimes the last thing she wants to do is go to sleep."

"D.J.'s wife, Allaire, told me the same thing about their little boy."

"You said he's two, right?" Erika asked as they climbed the staircase to Emilia's room.

"Yes. A couple of months older than Emilia."

"And your cousin Dax has children, too?"

"His wife, Shandie, had a little girl when they married, but Dax is as bonded to her as he is to his son."

Emilia was babbling now to herself and Erika kissed her little girl's cheek.

Dillon felt a band of painful longing tighten around his heart.

Emilia's room was painted yellow. There were cutouts of Winnie the Pooh, Tigger and Eeyore on the walls. Dillon felt as if he had no right to be part of this nightly ritual, but the urge to watch mother and daughter was strong and he leaned against the doorway.

Erika was totally caught up in changing Emilia…and slipping her little nightshirt decorated with lollipops over her head. All the while, she spoke to her. "Soon we'll have to find you some pj's with footsies."

"She'll probably enjoy the snow this year," Dillon offered, suddenly needing to be part of the conversation, not wanting to feel like an outsider.

Erika tossed a look over her shoulder as she sat Emilia on the changing table, holding onto her at her waist. "She'll be fascinated by it," Erika agreed. "And I can't wait for the holidays. She'll be able to dip her hands in the cookie dough, notice the angel on top of the tree and maybe understand a little of the magic of the season."

"You still find it magical?"

Erika nodded, then added, "And holy."

The true meaning of Christmas had fallen by the wayside for Dillon. Since Toby had died and Megan had left, all the holiday meant was a dinner with his mother and Peter and his brothers and sister. But suddenly, standing here with Erika and her little girl, he saw even *that* dinner in a different light. A family was bigger than the sum of its individual parts, much bigger. Maybe his resentful feelings about Peter had been one more element that had marred his marriage and his feelings about his family for too many years.

As Erika carried Emilia to her crib, she said, "You look as if you're deep in thought."

"Not too deep," he returned nonchalantly, but he could see she wasn't buying it.

She took a stuffed dog from the corner of the crib and handed it to Emilia. Her daughter tucked the dog into her body like the precious comfort that it was.

"Can you say good-night to Dr. Dillon?" Erika asked her.

Emilia held on to the crib railing, rocking back and forth from one foot to the other. Then she smiled at him and said, "Nighty-night, Dr. Diwwon."

The tug toward mother and child was so strong Dillon couldn't resist. Crossing to them, he gave Emilia a good-night hug. "Nighty-night, little one." Then in turmoil because of conflicting emotions, he said, "I'll wait downstairs," and left the nursery.

Fifteen minutes later, he'd straightened the books on the coffee table and righted the cushions on the sofa. Erika descended the stairs, adjusted the baby monitor on the side table and sank down on the couch a few inches away from him.

"Thank you," she said, motioning to the room. "You didn't have to straighten up."

"I needed something to do."

"You'd be handy to have around," she teased.

A hushed quiet fell between them as their gazes locked and both thought about what she'd said.

"Would you like something to drink?" she asked. "I don't have anything hard, but I have soft drinks and juice."

"No, I'm fine." He leaned forward, clasped his hands and dropped them between his knees.

She moved a little closer to him until their arms were brushing. "Why did you come over tonight?"

"I wanted to see you outside of our work atmosphere again…somewhere other than on my turf."

"Why? To see if I'm the same person at work *and* at home?"

He shrugged. "Maybe. Maybe I wanted to see if *I* was the same person. Sitting here with you now with Emilia's toys all around feels a little different than talking to you in my office."

"This is my real life, Dillon, the one that matters. I need my job and I'll always do the very best I can, but Emilia is the center of my world."

"That's the thing about kids. They are *the* center and if that center collapses, so does the rest of a parent's world."

"You sound as if you know."

"I do."

Her eyes questioned him before she asked gently, "What happened?"

Did he want to talk about this? No. He rarely did—only when he was pushed by Corey or Zane. Maybe that's why it still seemed so raw. Maybe that's why the thought of being a dad again was so difficult to consider.

"Dillon?" Erika prodded.

He let out a deep breath. "I was married and had a little boy—Toby."

Erika studied him with a sympathy that almost halted his words. This was just so damn hard to talk about. Looking away from her, he spotted a toy car under a table and concentrated on that. "I met Megan when I was doing my residency. We dated for a year and decided to get married. I had warned her about residency and the grueling hours. I'm not sure now what she thought would happen if she got pregnant. Maybe she really believed we'd live on my inheritance or I'd join Ethan at Traub Industries and give up being a doctor. But she stopped taking her birth-control pills without telling me."

"She got pregnant?" Erika guessed.

Dillon nodded and blew out a breath. "Yes. Her stopping the pills damaged the sense of trust in our marriage. My reaction didn't help. I was furious for a while. But I wanted our baby. I loved her. I had just expected to wait to have a family until I was established in a practice. Toby was born at the end of my residency. Megan hired a nanny and I thought everything would be okay."

Erika covered his hand with hers. She squeezed his fingers and he brought his gaze back to her. "Our marriage wasn't okay. I joined a practice and that took more of my time than she ever imagined. When I *was* home, I spent time with Toby. But Megan and I hardly talked. We'd finally managed a routine and Megan and I were trying to take one night a week for ourselves—to pull our marriage back together again—when Toby got sick. It started with lethargy and bruising. If I had been home more...around him more, maybe I would have caught on sooner. But he was diagnosed with a rare type of leukemia."

"Oh, Dillon," Erika murmured, perhaps knowing what was coming.

"We took him to New York and L.A. The best doctors. The most cutting-edge therapies. But he died when he was four and a half and I could do nothing about it. Absolutely nothing."

Moving closer to him, Erika said, "I'm so sorry. I can't even imagine your heartache." Then she asked, "Do you have a picture of him?"

The question made the hole in his heart feel bigger. Still, he shifted on the sofa and pulled out his wallet. Then he extracted the photo of Toby hidden behind his driver's license.

Erika studied the photo of Toby when he was three, his blond hair gleaming in sunlight as he stood with a stubby bat in his hand, ready to swat a ball that came his way.

"I hope that's how you remember him."

Dillon carefully inserted the photo back in his wallet. "It's complicated. I wasn't around as much as I should have been before he was diagnosed. So most of our time together was when he was sick. Unfortunately, I can't choose to remember only the good times."

"You and your wife didn't turn to each other?"

"Actually we did in a way…during his illness. I took a leave of absence. We supported each other and Toby the best way we knew how. But afterward, something was broken. Maybe *we* were broken."

"Your hearts were broken," Erika said quickly.

"I guess I wanted to go back to practicing medicine to give my life purpose. Something to do everyday that mattered. But when I returned, I still had long hours. And too much had gone wrong." He sighed. "Megan and I divorced two years ago."

"Did you take a leave from your practice to come up here?"

"After Megan and I separated, I took a wilderness survival course up here with vacation days and decided to apply for my license in Montana. My contract with the practice in Midland is up for renewal, and I told Marshall that when I was here in June. That's why he asked me to step in for him."

"So I guess you have a decision to make at the end of the month."

"Yes, I do."

They sat in silence for a few minutes until Erika said, "I can understand if you find being with children...being with Emilia...difficult. Now I understand why you look at Emilia the way you do, as if she brings you joy and pain at the same time."

His silence was his response until finally he nodded.

Disentangling their hands, he slid his arm around her shoulders, wanting the contact, needing to touch her. They sat in silence for a short while, then he admitted, "I like being with you."

"I like being with you, too," she replied almost shyly. "But if I see you, Dillon, if I spend time with you, if I let Emilia get attached to you, what happens to the two of us when you leave?"

"Don't you think the only way to figure it out is if we see each other, spend real time together and figure out each day as it comes?" He breathed in the scent of her, felt the warmth of her skin under her sweater, knew in his gut his attraction to Erika went deeper than his body's response to her.

When she tipped her chin up, her hair fell across her brow, her eyes glistened with emotion. "The idea of spending time with you terrifies me because I already like you and I feel as if I'm falling—" She abruptly stopped.

Dillon stroked his fingers through her hair, then he placed the gentlest of kisses on her lips. It was nothing like the others they'd shared. It was just a taste. *She* would have to decide how much more she wanted.

She looked bemused as he leaned away.

After a few moments, he broke eye contact and stood. "This is a decision you're going to have to make, without any pressure from me. I understand Emilia is your most important concern. But how you choose to live your life will teach her how to live hers. In the long run, the safe route isn't always safe at all. Sometimes it's a dead end. Maybe we both need to take a risk."

"You act as if this is a simple decision," she murmured, her voice a little shaky.

"It's not simple, but it is a decision." He pulled his hand to his side…away from her hair…away from her beautiful face…away from her body that he longed to touch.

Just what would Erika's decision be?

A half hour later, Dillon let himself into his suite and went to his bedroom. Saying goodbye to Erika had been tough. He knew he had to stand back and let her make up her mind. Hell, he didn't know if *he* was ready for an involvement…short *or* long.

He'd just changed into sleeping shorts when his cell phone chimed. Taking it from the dresser, he glanced at the ID and smiled when he recognized Zane's number.

Instead of a greeting, Dillon said, "I hear you're coming to my neck of the woods."

Zane chuckled. "Since when is Montana *your* neck of the woods?"

Dillon sank down onto his bed, suddenly wondering that himself. Maybe it had been a Freudian slip. "I've been here two weeks and I'm settling in, but I think I'd prefer a log cabin to my luxury suite. It has everything I need, but sometimes maybe I don't want everything I need. Do you know what I mean?"

"I know exactly what you mean. The public thinks being waited on hand and foot is a good thing, but it makes a guy lazy. That's why I hole up at my homestead off a not-very-traveled road."

Zane had bought a small stone house in Utah with a lot of land for privacy's sake. Very few people knew about it.

"My manager was impressed with Miss Rodriguez," Zane said. "After his initial acceptance, she called him with all the organizational stuff she needed to know. Very thorough."

"Erika is definitely conscientious and thorough."

"Do you know her well?" Zane's tone was patently curious.

"I'm getting to know her better each day." There was no point beating around the bush with Zane. Once Zane arrived, he'd see the electricity between the two of them.

"Is it serious?"

"We're both fighting it. I have a career and a life in Texas, she has a history with a bad relationship and a little girl to show for it."

"How old's her little girl?" Zane always went straight to the point.

"Emilia's almost two...absolutely adorable."

"How do you feel about being around her?"

A long silence stretched between them until Zane said, "Life is full of all kinds of pain, Dillon, but I'm not sure you can resist it. It's part of life. It makes us who we are. You have to learn to balance it with the joy."

Dillon had missed Zane poking into his life. "It'll be good to see you again. It's been too long."

"Yeah, it has. It will be crazy when I'm there. We can only spare about thirty hours out of my schedule. But somehow, you and I are at least going to have a beer together."

"That sounds good. Call me when your bus rolls through Bozeman."

"Will do."

Dillon put down his phone, staring at it for a few moments. It had been a while since he'd heard Zane strum his guitar.

It had been a while since he'd let Zane dig up the past. However, maybe his friend could give him a bead on his growing attachment to Erika.

Still…did Dillon *really* want his good friend's perspective on what he should or shouldn't do?

Chapter Seven

Erika exchanged a glance with Dillon the following afternoon as they sat in his office with Grant Clifton, who had asked to see them. Just that brief meeting of their eyes felt like a fall into space. When he'd said good-bye to her the night before, she hadn't known what the future would bring them. Wasn't she opening the door to heartache by making her heart vulnerable again?

She tried to concentrate on Grant. The resort manager was tall and lean and always seemed happy these days, most likely because his wife, Stephanie, was pregnant.

Grant spoke first. "We averted disaster with Mr. Lindstrom and his son thanks to both of you. Now I'd like to do a little more so food allergies aren't a problem in the future. Dillon, I'd like you to give a workshop tomorrow to all the employees of the restaurants in the resort about the importance of food prep and handling of special requests."

Dillon considered it. "You're thinking if the chefs and servers are all more educated on the subject, they'll be more careful."

"Exactly," Grant agreed. "I want them to realize they need to stay updated and alert. If a guest asks for a special dinner, there's probably a good reason why. It's not a whim."

Grant addressed Erika. "The reason I wanted you here is because I'd like you to assist Dillon. I know this is short notice and he'll need secretarial help."

Erika waited, expecting him to explain, and he did.

"I'd like you to make a list of the employees, make sure each will be there, even if you have to offer a personal invitation. At the workshop, I'd like you to hand out the information Dillon puts together and just generally make sure all goes smoothly. I know you're wearing more than one hat right now…and Frontier Days are approaching in a week and a half. If you don't think you can fit this in, I'll find someone else to do it."

"Oh, I can fit it in," she said quickly, without even thinking about it.

Across his desk, Dillon frowned. Because he knew about the class she was taking? About how little sleep she must be getting?

"I sent memos to the restaurants telling them about the workshop from two to three in between service breaks. If there are employees who absolutely can't make it, we can still give them the information and make sure they attend a workshop later. When Marshall returns, he can follow up with what you've done."

Grant addressed Erika again. "I've been told you're a detail person. Even the mayor had good things to say about you, so I'm sure I can count on you to make sure nothing goes unattended."

"Yes, sir, you can."

"Great. Neither of you have to walk me out. I know my way." With a grin, he stood and left Dillon's office.

But Dillon wasn't smiling when Erika turned to face him, asking, "What's wrong?"

He was silent for a while as if debating with himself whether he should say anything or not. Then he asked, "Did you really need something else to do? Maybe you should have told Grant that every spare minute in your day is already taken."

"And maybe the work I do is my concern and not yours."

"Erika, I see the dark circles under your eyes. I know your time with Emilia is limited as it is. Yes, the promotion means a lot to you, but I don't think you need to do this to earn a promotion. Coordinating Frontier Days should do that."

She rose from her seat, shaking her head. If she didn't combat his protective streak, his caring would get to her and she couldn't let it. "I'll take all the responsibility I can get if that means it will cement my position here and earn me a raise."

"I can have someone else type up lists," he insisted, pushing back his chair, joining her where she stood. The buzz between them vibrated like a live wire.

Finally she sighed. "I know you can. But I'll e-mail each employee personally and follow up with a call. I'll do this right, Dillon. You know I will."

She knew she should step away from him, but she didn't. She stood her ground and that was her mistake.

He spoke softly, but his words carried a whopping

impact. "I care about you, Erika…and Emilia, too. We haven't known each other very long, but—" He reached out, touched a few of the waves in her ponytail, then dropped his hand to his side. "But time doesn't always make a difference in something like this."

He had no right to sound as if her life mattered to him. He had no right to pluck a chord inside of her that wanted to sing. In spite of herself, she remembered her months with Scott and couldn't help comparing that time to now…couldn't help comparing him to Dillon. They were both well-off men with a way with women. That's what confused her so about Dillon. Did he act this way with all women, or just with her?

"Last night you said I had to make a decision," she responded. "I'm not ready to do that. I'm still trying to absorb everything you told me. I think I need some time and space."

"I can give you space. But maybe not time."

And that was the crux of her dilemma.

She took a deep breath. "I'd better start on that list."

Then she turned away from the caring as well as the desire in his eyes and left his office.

Erika stood at the door of the conference room the following afternoon, distributing Dillon's handouts to the employees coming in to hear his presentation.

She nodded and smiled to everyone and tried not to feel paranoid when she felt gazes on her. They were interested in the seminar, not in her. At least that's what she told herself until two women, who looked to be about her age, began whispering as soon as they passed her. She heard one say to the other, "I heard she's more than Dr. Traub's receptionist. Joanne saw them in the parking lot one night last week. Their lips were locked tight. Maybe he's her next sugar daddy."

The night of the potluck supper, Erika had thought no one else had been in the parking lot. But then it had been dark and she hadn't looked around until after she'd pulled away from Dillon's embrace.

So everyone was thinking she took up with Dillon because she wanted a replacement for Scott? Hadn't she proven she could be a good employee and a good mother? Why did gossip have to be so easy, and putting out the fires from its effects so hard? She fought back tears, attempting to maintain her professional composure.

A few minutes later she finally felt as if she'd regained her equilibrium. And that was a good thing because Dillon came walking down the hall toward her. He stopped. "You've done a great job pulling this together."

She glanced around, saw the women who had gossiped watching and felt suppressed emotion make her chin quiver. "It was my job." She tried to keep her voice even.

Dillon must have seen the quiver in her chin. "Are you upset about something?"

"No." She swallowed hard and blinked fast. Checking her watch, she advised him, "You'd better get started. They have to return to the restaurants to prepare for dinner."

"Tell me what happened, Erika. Something obviously did. You're near tears."

She cleared her throat and looked down at her high heels so he wouldn't see the tears swimming in her eyes. "Don't worry about me. Just do what you came here to do."

Knowing she couldn't stand there with him any longer, knowing there were some people watching, knowing she would be food for gossip again tomorrow if she didn't make a getaway, she handed him the rest of the papers.

"Don't come after me," she said in a desperate whisper. "Don't make this worse." Then she headed for the ladies' room down the hall, not intending to emerge until her makeup was perfect and her professional facade was back in place.

Dillon didn't know what to think as he watched Erika walk away. She had pride. He could see that in the set of her shoulders. But she was upset, too, and that had been obvious in her shaky words, in her bright eyes and the way she'd hurried away. If it hadn't been for her plea for him not to follow her, he would have, meeting or no meeting. He'd respect her wishes for now, but as soon as this presentation was over, he'd find her.

Speaking before a group had never bothered Dillon, so he took his place at the podium and let Grant introduce him. Then he launched into a presentation on the most common food allergies, who was most affected and what precautions the staff needed to take. He allowed plenty of time for questions and there were quite a few. All the while, though, he had Erika on his mind, too, and the vision of her straight back as she rushed down the hall.

He was worried about her. So when the hour-long workshop was over, he left the conference room and headed back to the office. He assumed that's where she'd be. But when he returned, she wasn't sitting at her desk in the reception area and he found Ruthann covering the phone and any emergencies that might crop up.

"Hey, Doc. How'd it go?" she asked.

"I think it was successful. Have you seen Erika?"

"She was here for a little while, but then she popped in to tell me she needed to make a call. I'm not sure where she went to do that. That was about ten minutes ago."

Make a call. Maybe she was calling a friend to talk about whatever had happened to her. Where would she go to make that call? "I'm going to step out for a little while," he told Ruthann. "You have my cell-phone number if you need me."

She nodded. "Sure do," then with a wink, she said, "I hope you find her."

He couldn't be that transparent, could he?

After he thought about Erika's options, he dismissed the route through the lobby that led to the boutiques. If she wanted quiet, she wouldn't go that way. He took the hall that led to the back of the building and went down a flight of stairs. Instead of heading into the underground garage, he pushed through the door that led outside to a garden and a fantastic view of the mountains. September was coming into its glory. The purple peaks wore a caplet of snow. Brilliant blue sky, populated by a line of puffy white clouds, was one of the reasons tourists visited here. But in spite of the vista before him with its pines, golden hills and autumn-dressed trees, his gaze fell on the beautiful woman sitting on an outcropping of rock a few feet below him. She was using her cell phone.

He let the door close quietly behind him so as not to startle her. But she must have heard him. The smile faded from her lips and he heard her say, "I'll talk to you in a little while, baby. Give the phone to Grandma."

Emilia must have done as Erika asked because Erika said, "I have soup in the slow cooker. If you'd like to join us for supper, you're welcome. Okay, I'll see you around five-thirty."

Erika closed her phone but didn't rise from her perch. So Dillon did the only sensible thing. He joined her. "You're going to get your suit dirty," he said matter-of-factly.

"You will, too."

"I guess we'll both have to send our clothes to the dry cleaners. Making plans for supper?"

"My mother knows I want to be on my own, so she doesn't intrude. But it's nice to have family around you, you know?"

"Is that why you wanted to talk to Emilia—you needed to have family around you?"

"Emilia keeps me grounded."

The wind blew around them, whispering secrets, soothing away tension.

"Tell me what happened before the workshop," he prompted.

She remained silent. She hadn't looked at him since he'd sat down beside her. Now she still kept her gaze on the mountains and whatever else she saw in the distance. "There's gossip about us."

"What kind of gossip?"

"Someone saw us the night we kissed in the parking lot. Apparently rumors have been making the rounds."

He swore under his breath. "Aren't small towns just great?" Knowing his anger wouldn't help, he asked, "What did you hear?"

She didn't answer.

"Erika?"

Almost defiantly, she faced him. "They're saying that maybe you're my next sugar daddy."

That took him aback. "Because?" he prompted.

"Because Scott had plenty of money. And I...I fell for him fast. I guess they're making comparisons. On the surface, you and Scott are a lot alike."

Dillon felt the pulse in his temples throb. Annoyance, anger, resentment? He wasn't sure what he felt, but he did know why he felt it. "Are you making the same comparisons?"

When she was silent again, he cupped her elbow. "Erika, look at me."

She did, and her expression was troubled as he said, "You told me what happened with Scott. I understand the gossip. I know you want to protect Emilia. But I am *not* him. You and I are both being honest with each other. I know he wasn't honest with you. Maybe it's experience that's taught me a thing or two. I don't know. But I do know you have to face the gossip head on and hold your head up high. Neither of us has done anything wrong."

She bit her lower lip and shook her head. "I understand that, but I guess I was worried...I was worried you'd believe the gossip."

"That you're a gold digger?"

She nodded again and a tear fell down her cheek. He couldn't keep from wrapping his arm around her. He couldn't keep from pulling her into his shoulder. He couldn't keep from holding her tight. "You're not a gold digger. I know that."

She tilted her head up. "How can you be so sure? As you said, we haven't known each other very long."

"I've seen you with Emilia. I've seen how hard you work. I know how much you've been battling not to be involved with me."

Apparently playing devil's advocate, she suggested

drily, "Maybe all that's a show, just to pique your curiosity so you're more interested."

"You forget, I'm a doctor. I see patients most days and I have to guess or intuit what's going on. I'm a good judge of character, Erika. If I ever could convince you to go on a date with me, I don't think you'd expect a new car at the end of the evening."

She laughed at that wild scenario. "Oh, Dillon, you make it all sound so foolish."

"Not foolish. I know what other people say can hurt. But you have to let it slide off of you."

"What happened with Scott filled me with insecurities. It's been hard to regain my own self-respect, let alone the respect of others." She looked up at him with those sparkling brown eyes that practically took his breath away. "But when I'm sitting here with you like this," she went on, "I can believe what the rest of the world thinks doesn't matter."

Where they were sitting, no one could see them. It was just the two of them and the mountains and the wonderful blue sky. He bent his head and gently but possessively took her lips. She responded by opening them to him. He searched her mouth for the passion that had lighted so easily with them…and he found it. Soon they were both breathing hard and not from the altitude.

Eventually he broke away and rested his forehead against hers. "Why don't you take the rest of the afternoon off. You worked extra hours on the workshop info."

"I don't want special perks because you're my boss."

"No special perks, just comp time. I know you're putting in more hours than you should on Frontier Days."

He dropped his arm from her, rose to his feet, but held out his hand to help her up. When she took it, he felt he had jumped a major hurdle. He felt Erika had finally confided in him and trusted him.

Now what was he going to do with that trust?

The infirmary suite was quiet a few hours later as Dillon sat at his computer. Suddenly there was a rap on his door and a familiar male voice inquired, "Is there a doctor in the house?"

Dillon grinned as his cousin D.J. walked in. He wore a sweatshirt and jeans and didn't look anything like the rich man he was.

"There definitely is a doctor in the house. Whenever I've stopped by the Rib Shack you haven't been there."

D.J. shrugged. "The manager's great. I stop in at least once a day and make sure the quality of the food and service is up to par. But with Allaire teaching, time with her and Alex is precious."

D.J. and Allaire had been best friends in high school, but then D.J.'s brother, Dax, had come along and swept her off her feet for a while. After she and Dax divorced, D.J. returned to town, finding his unrequited love was now returned. They'd been married for three years and were definitely each other's soul mates.

D.J. produced foam containers from his bag, set one in front of Dillon and one in front of himself. "I figured you'd be working through dinner. That's country-fried steak with corn bread, gravy, green beans and smashed potatoes. I know you like the ribs, but this is good, too."

Dillon opened the container and the aroma from the freshly made food made his stomach grumble. "I'm glad you stopped, food or no food. I intended to get out to your place again, but I think this month is going to speed by."

"That's why I'm here, to offer you a special invitation. Allaire thinks you need some home cooking and downtime. She says with being on call twenty-four hours a day, you're stressed and don't know it. So she wants you to come out to the ranch on Saturday and stay overnight. Babchek will cover for you, won't he?"

"I don't know. I'll have to check with him and Ruthann, too."

"So check and let us know." After a short pause and few bites of his steak, D.J. added, "Allaire said you could bring a guest if you want."

Dillon cut D.J. a sharp glance. "A guest?"

"Rumor has it that a certain pretty receptionist was caught kissing you in the parking lot."

"I can't believe Erika was right about the gossip."

"She heard it?"

"Today. She was upset."

"Is it true?" D.J. prodded.

"About the parking lot? I was kissing her, and she was kissing me back," he replied succinctly.

"If the gossip had been about Corey, I would have believed it right away. You? Not so much. This isn't like you. You'll be going back to Texas, won't you?"

"Truthfully, I'm not sure what I'll be doing."

"Is there sizzle between you two?"

"There's sizzle."

D.J. grinned at him. "So ask her to come to the ranch with you."

"I doubt if she'll leave her daughter for the weekend."

"She can bring her little girl along. I'm sure Dax will

be over with Kayla and Max. The kids will have a ball.
Run it by her and see what she says."

Dillon thought about their last kiss and wondered
himself what Erika would say....

Chapter Eight

Erika sat in D.J. and Allaire's living room, feeling in a way as if she'd landed on another planet. When Dillon had asked her to join him here this weekend, she'd remembered how she had confided in him about the gossip…how she'd trusted him. She was confused about her growing feelings for him, but she hoped spending more time with him would ease that confusion. After all, they wouldn't be alone here together. What could happen?

The ranch house was huge and lovely. Allaire's artistic touches were everywhere—from a painting on the living room wall, to the pictures of their little boy, Alex, which were set off in beautiful, hand-painted frames. The couple had welcomed her into their home as if she were an old friend. Dax and Shandie were warm and friendly, too. It was easy to see the bond between the two brothers even though Erika had heard their relationship had been rocky until recently. Watching from the sidelines, she felt the affection among the cousins as they cracked jokes and held interested conversations. They were all wonderful with the children... including Emilia.

Erika supposed what made her feel the most strange was studying these three men who obviously enjoyed caring for children. Had her father and Scott been the exception, not the rule? Or were D.J., Dax and Dillon rare finds?

The sense of family these three men shared was a bit awe-inspiring. Their connection shouldn't create more conflict within her, but for some reason it did.

Was it real? was the question that screamed inside her head. *Could it last?* was the question that followed.

Dillon finished speaking with Dax and came to sit beside her on the colorful patchwork sofa. Kayla—Dax and Shandie's daughter—had corralled Emilia and was sitting beside the beautiful stone fireplace with her, playing with the busy box Dillon had given her.

As Dillon leaned close to Erika, he murmured into her ear, "What's going through that pretty head of yours?"

"How do you know anything is?" she teased.

He touched the tip of his finger to her lower lip. "Because you bite your lip, and your brow furrows, and you push your hair over your shoulder. That's how I can tell you're thinking."

His words caught her totally off guard. No man had ever analyzed her so well. Yes, she knew those were her habits, but no one had cared to notice them before.

"You look shocked," he said in a low voice. "Why? Don't you think I watch you when you talk to me, when you're busy, when you're worried?" He bumped her shoulder. "I, of course, have no telltale idiosyncrasies."

"Oh, yes, you do," she protested. She touched the middle of his forehead with her index finger. "You get one very big furrow right there." Then she stroked right below his temple by both eyes. "And here, the little lines become deeper." She brushed the muscle along his neck. "When you're really upset or disturbed by something, this pulses."

By the time she was finished, she knew neither of them should be touching each other in this public setting because they were setting off signals, igniting sparks, inciting intimacy that couldn't be continued here.

"So I guess we both read each other pretty well," Dillon suggested huskily.

"Maybe. But all of that's just on the surface. We can't see the real feelings inside."

"Maybe not," he agreed. "But if you use clues, you'll always find the answer to the mystery."

"The same way you diagnose?" she asked.

"Sort of. So tell me what you were trying to diagnose before I came over."

She suddenly felt as if those thoughts were private territory, not something Dillon could help her with. On the other hand, maybe he could clear them up. "Do Dax and D.J. act like fathers all the time?"

"Do you mean are they putting on a show for your benefit?"

"Exactly."

"They're fathers all the time. They have as much care of their kids as their wives do. They have to. Both of their wives work."

"I know Allaire teaches high school. I don't know much about Shandie."

"She's a hairdresser. She's part owner of Clip N' Curl Salon. She and Dax juggle their schedules to take care of the baby. Kayla's in first grade so they have some leeway there. Allaire and D.J. do the same." He paused for a moment then added, "And Allaire and Shandie both had to face gossip in their lives. I'm not going to tell you about it, because I think they should. I think you have a lot in common with them."

Did she? Had these beautiful, confident, loving women had to face what she'd faced? Dillon dropped his arm around her shoulders and gave her a squeeze. She did like the feeling of belonging that gave her. They were here as a couple and in spite of everything, that felt right. Yet she couldn't let herself get too used to it. She couldn't depend on the slippery hope that it would continue to feel right.

So for that reason, she moved away from Dillon and rose to her feet. "I'd better see if Allaire needs some help in the kitchen. I can't believe she prepared supper for everyone herself." Erika knew they were having meat loaf and mashed potatoes, hot wings and vegetable casseroles. Wanting to do her part, she had brought a batch of oatmeal cookies for the kids and Waldorf salad for the adults.

"Allaire likes to cook, and I'm sure D.J. didn't let her do those wings all by herself. Not with his secret barbecue sauce recipe."

Erika had difficulty moving away from Dillon. She so liked being with him, sitting close, feeling as if they belonged together. But she crossed the room and stopped to talk to Kayla, to make sure she didn't mind playing with Emilia. The two little girls seemed to be having a good time so Erika went to the kitchen. When she stole a last glance at Dillon, he was watching two-year-old

Max with his dad. Was he sad? Was he remembering Toby? Would he consider being a dad again?

In the kitchen, Erika was struck by the beauty of the granite counters and island, the white cupboards hand-painted with a flower pattern that had the flair of Allaire's strokes. "What can I do to help?" she asked Allaire.

D.J.'s wife was garnishing a tray of celery and carrot sticks with cherry tomatoes. "I think we're good. It's not quite time to boil the potatoes. I just put the meat loaves in the oven. D.J. said not to touch his wings in the slow cooker."

Erika smiled and slipped onto one of the high bar stools at the island.

Allaire slid the tray of vegetables into the large, side-by-side refrigerator. Then she asked Erika, "Iced tea?"

"That sounds good."

Allaire poured them two glasses and sat at the island with her. "I'm glad Dillon brought you here this weekend."

Erika tilted her head and waited.

Allaire's beautiful blue eyes were kind as she said, "Dillon needs someone like you."

"Someone like me?"

Allaire looked a bit flustered. "I pretty much say what I think. Is that all right with you?"

"Yes, it is. I'd much rather know what a person's thinking than guess."

"Good. That's the way I feel. So when I said a person like you, I meant a woman who has it all together, who's very attractive, but who also has a child."

"I don't think he wants to be around children."

Allaire smiled. "I'm not sure about that. Dillon's

daddy material and deep down, he knows it. He's been running from relationships and putting all of his energy into his practice as an escape. I think he's sidestepped real involvement."

She took a swallow of her tea then went on. "I noticed he's good with Emilia. And Emilia seems to gravitate toward him. That's what he needs to bring him back to life."

"But he'll be leaving in a couple of weeks."

"Will he?" Allaire asked.

What did Allaire mean—*was* there a chance Dillon would stay on in Montana? Was there a chance he'd ask her to go back to Texas with him? Should she even consider such a huge life change for a man? She'd never known a man who was worthy of that kind of risk, especially one who wasn't sure he wanted a real family again.

All of the questions swirled in her head until she couldn't seem to clear it.

Suddenly she needed an escape for a little while, but not before she found out something she needed to know. "I went through a lot of scandal as a pregnant single mom, and choosing a man who didn't want to be a dad. Dillon seemed to think you'd understand that."

"Oh, I understand. Talk about scandal. I was the perfect daughter and the perfect wife...until I wasn't. My marriage to Dax just didn't work out, and the end of our relationship was food for the rumor mill. When I hooked up with D.J. again, tongues wagged. In fact, they could have torn me and D.J. apart, but we didn't let them. Gossip runs rampant in a town like Thunder Canyon. You've just got to walk away from it and hope that soon they start gossiping about something else."

Walk away from it. That was a good way to put it.

"I've never been on a ranch before. Is it all right if I take a walk down to the barn and check out your horses?"

"Sure. I'll keep an eye on Emilia for you."

"Thanks, I really appreciate it. I won't be long."

She just needed some fresh air to put everything she'd seen and heard into some kind of perspective.

The huge red barn was foreign territory to her. But she loved the big sky and lots-of-land feel of the place. The fresh air, the aspens and oaks, the fir groves here and there, along with the scent of sage, the cooking smells wafting outside and the sound of horses cavorting in pens urged her to feel free. She could see how after living out here on a place like this, town could seem constricted.

Yet she also knew it wasn't merely a place that could make her constricted or free, but rather the life she chose for herself and the way she felt about it.

Erika heard the thump of Dillon's boots before she saw him. His ribs were healing and not affecting his daily life. He looked like a down-home cowboy today in his snap-button shirt, jeans and boots that appeared as if they'd seen some work. He'd worn a Stetson when he'd picked her up and she'd smiled. She'd asked if he'd bought it just for today. He'd laughed in return, and said, "No, it's mine. I just don't wear it much when I'm treating patients."

That had been another moment when Erika had realized she didn't know everything about Dillon. She probably didn't even know half.

"Do you want to go inside?" he asked, seeing her at the side door to the barn. "A few horses are already inside for the night."

"Oh, I don't know…"

"Afraid?" he asked with a sly grin.

"I'm not afraid of anything." Her shoulders went back and her chin came up. But when she stared into Dillon's eyes, she knew what she'd said wasn't true. She was still afraid of him, and what he could do to her heart.

"Come on, then," he invited, opening a huge door and letting her precede him inside.

The inside of the barn was cavernous and dark, yet the sounds of the horses huffing and pawing gave the place a homey feel.

After Dillon flipped on the lights, she noticed two rows of stalls faced each other. He stopped before a paint pony. "Did you come down here to get away from the crowd, or because something's bothering you?"

"Maybe a little of both. I don't have much family, just Mom and Emilia, so being with yours is a bit over-whelming. Enjoyable though," she added.

"Are you sure?"

"Yes. Being with everyone encouraged me to think about how I grew up...without an extended family... without a dad."

She studied the horse, tentatively stretched her hand out to him. He nosed at her fingers and she smiled. "After my father left and I didn't hear from him again, I thought I'd done something wrong, that he didn't love me and he never could."

Dillon leaned against the stall and his gaze lingered on hers. "Do you realize now it wasn't your fault?"

"On my good days."

When she didn't say more for a while, Dillon admit-ted, "When my stepfather came on the scene, I wanted my real dad back. The missing was already deep and dark and cutting. When Peter was around, it just seemed worse. My dad dying, and then my mom marrying Peter...that was all my first experience with something

I couldn't change and I became even more determined to change what I could. I guess that was another reason I wanted to be a doctor. Yet with Toby's illness, I learned again I didn't have control of much."

"We all like to think we have control over our lives... that we can protect loved ones."

They seemed to turn to each other simultaneously in understanding. She looked into Dillon's eyes and found him gazing into hers. They were both searching. For answers? For reassurance? For desire that was undercutting any and all emotions but the need to be kissing each other...touching each other?

Taking Erika's hand, Dillon tugged her a little way down the aisle into a vacant stall. They stepped inside onto the clean hay. Dillon pushed his fingers through her hair and held her face in his hands.

The hushed peace of the barn surrounded them, broken the next moment by a horse snorting, then a breeze blowing against a loose windowpane. The resounding awareness that they were a man and a woman, alone in a private place, surrounded them. The bond between them was growing, and so was their attraction.

Erika saw the desire in Dillon's eyes before he acted on it. His intention became hers. As he bent his head, she wrapped her arms around his neck. Each time Dillon kissed her, she expected—hoped—part of her heart would remain immune. She'd been hurt and she had a wide scar. She'd never expected to feel anything there again. But Dillon was changing all that, not only with his kisses, but his words, his actions. She knew she shouldn't let her guard down. She knew she should run in the opposite direction. But right now, with Dillon's hands in her hair, his lips on hers, she didn't want to be anywhere but in his arms.

Her hands wandered from his neck and played over the shoulders of his denim shirt. The material was thick so she inched her fingers under the collar, found the band of his T-shirt and traced her fingertips along the neck. His skin was as hot as the heat burning inside her belly.

Dillon must have been feeling the same need, because his hands passed down her back, stopped at the hem of her soft pink sweater, then slid underneath until his palms lay along her midriff.

"Are you okay with this?" he whispered into her ear.

"I'm more than okay," she said breathlessly.

Leaning back a bit, she moved her hands from his shoulders...down the placket of his shirt. She pulled his T-shirt from his jeans and slid her hands underneath and felt Dillon's stomach muscles tighten at her touch. She couldn't ever remember being quite this bold.

With Scott, sex had been serious business, and their dates usually ended in his bed. But Dillon didn't seem to be in any hurry, and neither was she. Once a couple had sex, everything could change...not necessarily for the better, in her experience. She wasn't ready for any change. Feeling desire for Dillon didn't have to lead to a burning crash—not if they went slow and easy. Not if she made sure she knew exactly what she was doing. They could play, couldn't they? Have fun and take some pleasure, and forget for a few minutes the burdens outside their doors?

"Oh, Dillon," she said, sifting her fingers into his chest hair, reveling in it. "You're bringing something so different into my life, I'm not sure what to do with it."

Reaching up under the front of her sweater, he covered her breast with his palm, taking their intimate play to a new level. "This scares me, Dillon," she managed to say, hardy able to breathe.

"What—my touching you?" he said, kissing her again.

"Not your touching me. The way I feel when you do."

Slowly he dropped his hand from beneath her sweater and she was sorry she'd said anything.

But he didn't look sorry. He just looked patient. "I don't want to scare you. And we do have to go back to the house or Allaire will send out a search party. She's very protective of her guests," he teased.

Erika laughed, lightness flowing through her genuine laugh that she felt had been dormant inside of her ever since Scott left.

Dillon straightened her sweater and she snapped a couple of the snaps on his shirt. "Do we look present-able?" he asked, quirking up a brow.

"We both look like we've been kissing." She reached up and stroked a touch of pink from his upper lip. "You're wearing my lipstick."

He ran his thumb along her chin. "And you have a little bit of beard scratch on you. Someone like Allaire could tell."

"They'll know anyway," Erika said wryly, one arm around Dillon's waist, his around hers.

"How will they know?" he asked.

"Women just do. With what Allaire and Shandie have been through, they'll see."

"Do you mind? Would you rather take a walk and then go back in?"

"A walk would be nice. But I want to make sure Emilia's behaving. And it's okay if your family knows. Allaire and Shandie aren't the type to gossip. They had enough gossip tossed around about them, so they wouldn't do it to me."

"I'm glad that's settled. That means I can kiss you whenever I want this weekend, and not worry about the consequences."

But they both would be worrying about the consequences. They could change each other's worlds.

And that was the scariest thought of all.

Chapter Nine

Dillon's heart and mind were in turmoil as he glanced at the closed door to Erika's bedroom and descended the stairs early Sunday morning before sunup. He hadn't slept much last night. His room was next to Erika's and he could hear her moving around…hear her bed creak… hear Emilia when she had awakened in the middle of the night, then had soon quieted probably because Erika had gone to her and soothed her. It wasn't only his time in the barn with Erika yesterday that had caused the conflict in him. Last evening he had carried Emilia to her room, her little arms around his neck. She'd smiled at him and kissed him on the cheek before he'd laid her in the crib. He could so easily become attached to that little girl, let alone her mother.

What he needed was a strong cup of coffee. Not that the coffee would help him make any decisions. Time just seemed to be moving too fast. Frontier Days would start on Friday. Then he'd be here another week and that was it.

Unless...

Should he consider moving his life because of an attraction? Because of tender feelings he felt for a child? Texas was his home. Yet when he gazed out at the mountains from his office, when he looked into Erika's eyes—

He'd reached the kitchen just as the sun was starting to pop up over the horizon. Angling around the island, heading for the coffeepot on the counter, he caught movement out on the deck. Going to the French doors, he spotted Erika wrapped in an afghan, looking toward the sunrise.

How long had she been down here?

She must have come down while he was in the shower or he would have heard her.

When he stepped out onto the deck, the sky was absolutely golden, streaked with pink and purple to the east and west of the sunrise. The peaks of the pines on D.J.'s property seemed to poke into the gold, making light rain over the whole backyard.

Erika shifted toward him, her profile backlit by the blazing sun. "I just stole down here for a few minutes."

Without speaking, he just went over and sat beside her, sharing the moment.

"It's remarkable, isn't it? There's so much beauty in these hills."

He knew Erika was talking about the sunrise, but he was thinking of other things that weren't as uplifting.

"What are you thinking?" she asked quietly.

Did he want to tell her? Erika was an optimistic woman. She'd had to be to turn her life around as she had. She saw her child as a gift and the beauty in the world the same way.

He liked to think *he* was an optimist, but he was a realist, too. "I'm thinking people come to Montana to find this beauty so they can take it back with them. It helps them deal with what isn't so beautiful in their lives."

"Is that what you did? You came here in the summers and what you saw and what you did carried you through the rest of the year?"

"Yeah, I think that was the case. But I'm also thinking about the guests who come and go home and forget about the sunrise because they have to deal with everyday problems."

"There are problems here, too," Erika offered. "You saw some of them when you came to the potluck supper with me—men and women losing their jobs because of this economy, single moms trying to make ends meet on one salary... Thunder Canyon isn't immune."

"No, I suppose it's not. I guess I was thinking about the mobile units I worked with in Houston. The refugees from Katrina who needed medical care. So often I wish I could do more as a doctor. So much is out of my hands."

"Like your son passing too young? Like your dad dying when he was in his prime?"

She'd gone straight to the core of it. "Yes. Sometimes I have questions that are just too big for answers."

Their chairs were close together and now she leaned toward him. "Did you ever consider joining Doctors Without Borders? Or just giving a few weeks to bring health care to children who need it instead of coming to a place like this to practice?"

He raised an eyebrow. "Do you feel me practicing medicine here isn't worthwhile?"

"I'm not saying that. But I think *you* believe you'd be doing more good somewhere else."

Was Erika right? Would a concierge practice just increase his frustration that he couldn't do more?

"You asked me if I want to manage a resort someday," she said. "I only want to manage a resort to prove I can. I want to add something like that to my résumé. But eventually what I'd really like to do is to work at a foundation where I can do some good."

Dillon reached out and took her hand, sliding his thumb back and forth against her knuckles. He felt a tremble run through her and knew he could create desire in her, just as she created it in him. "Sometimes I think you believe that we're very different, that we've come from different worlds. But I don't think we are."

"You're the heir to an oil fortune," she pointed out. "You can work anywhere you want, do whatever you want to do, go wherever you want to go. You don't even *have* to work, if you don't want to. That in itself makes us very different, Dillon."

Sometimes her preconceptions about him made him angry. "You don't think *I* need meaningful work to do, too? I became a doctor to make a difference." And becoming a doctor was part of the reason why his marriage had fallen apart.

Erika let out a sigh and pulled her hand away. "You'll never understand how it feels to not have enough in your wallet to buy food for your next meal. You'll never understand how a father can walk out because he didn't want the responsibility of staying. You'll never understand what it is to have a new life to take care of when you haven't taken very good care of yourself. We *are* very different, Dillon. And one of the main differences is in a couple of weeks you'll be going back to Texas and I'll be staying here."

What could he say to her? *I'm attracted to you but it's too soon to expect anything else? I want to take you to bed but I don't want the pain of loving and losing?* He remembered too well Megan's withdrawal because his hours were too long and his time with her too limited. She couldn't understand why he wanted to become a doctor when he had his inheritance from his dad to rely on. But all the money in the world couldn't save their son.

Although he'd only known Erika for two and a half weeks, he felt as if he'd known her for much longer. Yet he *was* a practical man. Especially after this conversation, he didn't believe Erika would expect him to give up medicine for her. For her *and* Emilia, he corrected himself.

Yet, knowing her for just two and a half weeks, how sure could he be about that?

Dillon's office was quiet all Monday afternoon. He cast a glance out to the reception area, knowing Erika's desk chair was empty. Dammit, he missed her and he didn't want to.

The drive home yesterday from D.J.'s had been awkward. So had their greeting this morning. This afternoon, she'd left for an appointment in town with Bo Clifton. That had added a layer of restlessness to the time Dillon had spent in his office this afternoon. He didn't know Bo well, but he did know one fact about him. He was a charmer...and a self-proclaimed renegade. That was one of the reasons he was running for mayor.

Dillon checked his watch. How long could Erika's meeting with Bo take? She had said she'd wanted to consult with him about when and where he'd be addressing the residents of Thunder Canyon on Friday afternoon. All that would take about fifteen minutes. She'd been gone two hours.

It was none of his business.

A half hour later he was still trying to convince himself of that when Bo and Erika sailed into his office. Bo raised a hand in greeting and Dillon rose from his desk, walking to the middle of the room to shake his hand.

"It's good to see you again," Bo said. They'd run into each other in June at the town barbecue.

"It's good to see you, too." Dillon glanced over at Erika. Today she'd worn her hair in a chignon with tendrils escaping around her face. In a long-sleeved silky blouse with a navy vest and skirt, she was beautiful. In fact, Bo was looking at her now, too, and Dillon didn't like the glint in his eye.

"Good luck with your candidacy," Dillon forced himself to say, returning his attention to Bo.

"I intend to add hard work and glad-handing to that luck. Erika was kind enough to be a test audience for my speech."

"It's really good," she said, coming closer to the two men. "It lays out all the ways he's going to make this town better."

"I thought you were meeting at campaign headquarters." Bo's office was downtown in a drugstore whose proprietor had just retired.

"Oh, we did," Bo assured him. "But I had business up here with Grant, so I told Erika I'd walk her in. She was really a big help with my speech and helped me clarify a couple of points. Who knows? After I become mayor,

I might have to steal her away from the resort and bring her into the mayor's office."

Erika beamed with pleasure at Bo's compliment.

"Well, I know you two probably have work to do and Grant doesn't like it when I keep him waiting," Bo said. "It was good to see you again, Dillon." He lightly touched Erika's arm. "I'll see you again on Friday."

"I'll be in the front row listening."

Bo gave her a smile that Dillon knew would melt most of his female constituents.

After Bo left, Dillon asked Erika, "Had you met Bo before today?"

"Not really. I had a couple of phone conversations with him. Why?"

"You two seem to get along well."

"He seems like a nice guy." She was looking at Dillon with puzzlement.

"Lots of women think he is."

"Are you trying to warn me away from him?"

"No, of course not," Dillon answered gruffly, and went back to his desk. He had no right to tell Erika whom she could and couldn't see. He had no rights at all where she was concerned.

And that nettled him most.

He couldn't help but glance at her when he got back to his desk. She was still standing there studying him, head tilted, tendrils floating around her face in a way that made him want to brush them back. She asked, "Is something wrong?"

"No." Yet he knew it was.

"Well, I'll see you later," Erika said, waiting to see if he had something to discuss with her.

But he didn't. "Later," he repeated.

She left his office.

Erika worked on the computer the rest of the afternoon and Dillon didn't interrupt her. He didn't go near her. Whenever he did, he was overcome by the desire to take her into his arms, kiss her and take her to bed. He hadn't wanted a woman like this in a very long time. He couldn't even remember wanting Megan like this. Their physical relationship had always been satisfactory, except near the end. But he'd never felt the kind of need he felt coming from Erika, or even within himself. And that made him uneasy.

When Erika stopped in to say goodbye around 5:00, Dillon was somewhat curt. She looked...hurt.

Dammit, he didn't want to hurt her.

There was only one thing to do. Go after her and attempt to explain. She was walking out of the reception area when Dillon caught up with her. She looked up at him and he could see the conflict in her eyes...could practically feel the emotion washing through her.

"What did I do wrong?" she asked.

"You didn't do anything wrong. I know I was a bear this afternoon."

"A quiet bear," she said, breaking into a little smile.

"What's your favorite takeout? I'll pick some up and bring it over and we'll have supper with Emilia."

"Are you sure you want to?"

He could see she was remembering their conversation from Sunday. He was, too. "Yes, I do."

"And Emilia?" she asked, knowing he had mixed feelings about spending time with her little girl.

"And with Emilia. I can't wall myself off from children forever."

"But that's what you try to do."

He didn't deny it. "I know. I'll try not to tonight."

Erika looked as if she wanted to ask what that meant, but she didn't. She just said, "Emilia likes the fried chicken from that little restaurant over on Pine Street. If you could pick up some, that would be great. I have veggies I can warm up and some potato casserole I had left over from last night. If you don't mind leftovers," she added.

"The truth is, I don't care what we eat—I just want to be with you and Emilia."

He didn't touch her, though he wanted to. He promised her nothing would happen here where they worked. He kept his promises.

But she laid her hand on his bicep, and the contact seared not only his arm but his very center. "Then I'll see you in a little while."

He watched Erika walk down the hall into the huge lobby and get lost in the people mingling there. He'd notice her in any size crowd. He'd know her from a mile away.

He wasn't going to think about shoulds or shouldn'ts tonight. He was just going to try to stay in the moment.

Stay in the moment.

When Dillon knocked on Erika's door, a box of chicken in hand, he heard Emilia crying inside.

When he rapped harder, Erika called, "It's open. Come in."

After he opened the door and stepped inside, he found Emilia seated on the living room floor, red-faced and crying, pounding her little fists on her knees. Erika was kneeling beside her, talking to her in a calm voice. But it didn't seem to be helping. He guessed the toy bin next to Emilia was the source of her frustration, though he didn't know why.

"I brought supper," he called, smiling at Emilia, hoping to break the thread of whatever was going on.

She glanced at him for a moment, stopped crying, but then a second later continued again.

Erika shook her head. "She's being stubborn tonight. She wanted to dump out the whole bin of toys and I told her she had to pick two."

"Can she count?" Dillon asked teasingly.

"That's the point. I'm trying to teach her," Erika replied with a smile.

The wailing continued at a high pitch until Dillon set the chicken on a side table and crouched down to the almost two-year-old. "Hey there, little princess, what's this all about?" He held out his hands to her, not knowing what she would do.

Emilia gave her mom a baleful glance, then lifted her arms to Dillon, hiccuping.

He picked her up and rose to his feet. "So you think you can play with more than one toy at a time?" He scooped up a doll that was two-sided. One side was a plain little girl, the other side was a princess. He wiggled the doll at Emilia's tummy. "Don't you think this will keep you busy for a while? Especially if we cut up chicken into tiny little pieces so you can try to eat it."

Now Emilia was smiling at him and grabbing for the doll. He turned it to the princess side. "A little princess always listens to her mommy, doesn't she?"

At the word *mommy* Emilia's gaze went to Erika.

Erika just shook her head, came over to the two of them and wiped a few tears from her daughter's cheek. "Okay, tell me your secret. I tried to get her interested in the doll and she wanted no part of it. She just wanted to empty her toy bin."

Dillon laughed. "Your daughter simply knows that I'm Dr. Prince Charming and I can do no wrong."

As soon as he said the words, he wished he could draw them back. Because he could do some wrong. He could hurt Erika and himself in the process. And here he was, holding her daughter, liking the feeling of being here with both of them.

"I thought you'd run in the other direction if you heard her crying."

"I don't scare that easily." Their gazes held and the current that always danced between them was stronger than ever.

Erika licked her lips, then took a deep breath.

Dillon felt as if he could use a couple of breaths of that crisp, fall air outside.

Then she asked, "Could you bring her into the kitchen and put her into her high chair? I just finished warming the potatoes. I'll pop the vegetables in the microwave."

Fifteen minutes later Erika had finely minced the vegetables with chicken and stirred it into the mashed potatoes. Dillon didn't want to start without her. "I can wrap the rest of the chicken and put it in the oven until you're finished feeding Emilia."

"I'm used to cold food," she joked.

He realized again how many sacrifices Erika had made for her daughter, and the ones she was still making. He was filled with the desire to make her life easier. Yet he knew she was too independent to accept help. He felt so protective of the two of them, and he still hadn't figured out why. He'd been around moms and kids and backed away from them before.

Was he finally ready to move forward with his life? And what exactly did that mean?

Going to the counter he poured two mugs of the coffee that Erika had brewed. He took his black but he knew she liked sugar and cream. He fixed hers, then took both the mugs to the table.

She glanced down at it with a look of surprise on her face.

"What?" he asked.

"I don't think I've ever had a man serve me coffee."

He stopped by her chair and clasped her shoulder. "You deserve to be served coffee...and a lot more."

The heat that rose in her cheeks seemed to rush through his whole body. They were stepping into dangerous territory, teetering on the edge of an attraction that could easily turn into an affair. He moved away from her and sat across from her at the table again and took a sip of scalding coffee.

Erika had returned her attention to Emilia again, giving her a last spoonful of potatoes, then shaking a colorful cereal onto her tray. Emilia reached for one of the little shapes and grinned at her mom.

Erika stood, went to the oven and removed the chicken with an oven mitt. She set it onto the table with the other casseroles. "Dig in."

Dillon filled his plate and began eating. Erika did the same. The silence between them was comfortable until she asked blandly, "So...what was going on with you this afternoon?"

"You haven't guessed?"

She wiped her fingers on a napkin. "No. I thought maybe something happened while I was gone."

Dillon took her hand across the table and linked his

fingers with hers. She didn't pull away. "What if I told you I was jealous of Bo Clifton?"

After a quiet moment of studying his face she asked, "Are you serious?"

He rubbed his thumb back and forth across her palm. "I suppose that's what it was. It was a foreign feeling, really. I just didn't like the fact that he was being so charming to you."

"Oh, Dillon. Don't you think I recognize the difference between Bo giving me a compliment and you giving me a compliment?"

"I hope you do."

"You need to give me a little more credit. You need to trust—" She stopped.

"I need to trust you? Do you trust me?"

For a moment he thought she was going to get up and run away, but then she admitted, "I'm beginning to."

The phone on Erika's kitchen counter rang.

He reluctantly pulled his fingers from hers.

"I could let my machine take it, but if it's my mom she'll wonder why I'm not answering. She knows I'm home."

He nodded, wishing they weren't constantly interrupted…wishing they'd have some quiet time just for the two of them, away from work and responsibilities.

Erika answered the phone. "Hi, Mom." After she listened for a little while she said, "Dillon's here, having dinner with us."

He didn't know if her mom went silent or if she did, but there seemed to be a long pause. Then Erika said brightly, "You can bring it over now. We don't mind. I'm positive. I'll be getting Emilia ready for bed soon. Okay." She put down the receiver.

"Your mom's coming over?"

"Yes. I'm sorry. I don't know if she'll stay—"

"Don't apologize. She cares about the two of you. Do you want me to leave?"

"Don't be silly."

He liked her immediate and spontaneous reaction. Rising from his chair, he crossed to her. "One of these days we're going to have time alone."

She moved a little closer to him and almost whispered, "And what will we do with it when we do?"

He circled her waist with his arms and pulled her tighter against him. "That will depend on you."

He rubbed his cheek against hers, kissed her sweetly and slowly, knowing he had to keep it light with Emilia sitting close by...with Erika's mother on the way over.

The doorbell rang and he broke away from her. She looked as if she wanted to stay in his arms and that's what he wanted, too. But wanting something and getting it were two different things. "I'll take Emilia from her high chair. Go ahead and get the door."

Erika gave him a last longing glance before she opened the door to her mother.

Constance came in and took in the scene with one assessing look. "Hello, Dr. Traub," she said as she entered the kitchen.

Dillon almost smiled at her formality. "Hello, Mrs. Rodriguez. It's good to see you again." He'd taken Emilia from her high chair and was wiping her face with a napkin.

"There's still some chicken, Mom, if you'd like to have some," Erika invited.

"Oh, no, I ate. I just wanted to give you this for Emilia. I finished it tonight." She handed Erika the bag she'd brought along.

Erika peeked inside and took out a corduroy jumper

that was decorated with embroidered pumpkins. "Oh, it's adorable." She hugged her mother. "Thank you so much. She'll look so cute in it." She held it up to Emilia and said, "What do you think?"

Emilia took the jumper, brought it to her face and laid her little head against it. Erika and Dillon both laughed.

Dillon said, "You do beautiful work."

"Thank you," Constance returned. "Sewing is my favorite hobby."

In the awkward silence that followed, Erika took Emilia from Dillon's arms. "I'm going to take her upstairs and put her to bed. It won't take long. I think she's already half asleep. Do you want to help?" Erika asked her mom.

"No, you go ahead. I'll have a cup of coffee with Dr. Traub."

"Dillon," Dillon said, hoping to make them both feel more comfortable.

After Erika went upstairs with a worried glance at the two of them, he poured a mug of coffee for Constance. She added milk and sugar and sat at the table across from him. "I suppose you and Erika work closely together...since she's your receptionist," Constance began.

"Not so closely. Erika has other responsibilities that keep her busy, too. She met with one of the candidates running for mayor this afternoon."

"You had work to discuss this evening?" her mother asked.

"No, we didn't."

Constance frowned. "So you're becoming friendly outside of work?"

"I enjoy spending time with your daughter."

"Erika told me you lost a child. That must have been terrible."

"Yes, it was. At first I thought being around Emilia would be...hard. But each time I'm around her..." He shrugged. "I think about my son, Toby. But I also see Emilia for who she is, and she makes me smile."

"And Erika? She makes you smile, too?"

"Erika is a very special woman."

"Who is much younger than you are."

This interrogation was getting uncomfortable but Dillon tried to keep his tone from becoming defensive. "After what she's been through, I think she's mature beyond her years."

"And you think you have common ground?" Constance asked.

Erika was coming down the steps when Constance asked the question. She said to her mother, "Mom, what are you doing?"

Constance looked from her daughter to Dillon. "I'm just asking questions both of you should be thinking about."

"No, you're prying."

Just from seeing Erika and Constance together, Dillon already knew they were close. They depended on each other. He didn't want to come between them. He knew the best thing he could do was to let mother and daughter discuss this.

Rising to his feet, he said, "I'd better get back to the resort. I don't like to be away too long even when Ruthann is covering."

"You don't have to go," Erika insisted.

"Yes, I do." Their gazes locked and Erika was the first to look away. "I'll walk you out," she murmured.

She followed him to the door and outside onto the

small porch. "I'm sorry she gave you the third degree."

He linked his arms around Erika and said simply, "Don't be. She's your mom and she cares what happens to you. That's a good thing."

"Don't tell me her questions didn't annoy you."

"They weren't questions I haven't already thought about." He leaned down and gave Erika a sound, if short, kiss. Then he whispered against her hair, "One of these days we'll be together without interruption."

But they both knew his time here was growing short. Erika hugged him as if she didn't want to let him go. That hug made tonight worthwhile. The memory of Emilia's smile made tonight worthwhile. Maybe he really was ready to move his life forward.

Maybe.

Chapter Ten

After Dillon's patient left late Wednesday morning, Dillon closed his office door and went to his wall of windows, peering out. The problem was he wasn't seeing. The little boy, who was four, had reminded him so much of Toby. When would the gut-wrenching pain stop? When would he be able to just remember his son with joy instead of sadness?

When you stop feeling guilty, a little voice in his head whispered.

He doubted he would ever stop feeling guilty. He doubted he would ever stop regretting what might have been.

The knock on his door startled him but he was glad to see Erika when she peeked in. She smiled as she waved a deli bag at him. "You have no appointments this afternoon and I have a lunch for two. How would you like to ride with me to the cabin I'm checking for Zane?

You can tell me if there's anything I should change or bring in."

The idea of some time in Erika's company sounded like sweet relief from his troubled thoughts, though Dillon couldn't say why. Maybe it was her vibrant energy, or the sparkle in her eyes. Maybe it was the chemistry between them that seemed to supersede anything else. "How did you know I could use lunch away from my desk?"

"Because I noticed your last patient leave. He reminded me an awful lot of the picture you showed me of your son."

"I'm not reminded of Toby every time I treat a four-year-old patient."

"Maybe not, but it looks to me as if you were this time."

Erika always gave him the truth and he couldn't fault her for that. "Do you always have to be so honest?"

"It's the way I live my life. I don't let anyone else try to pull the wool over my eyes and I don't do it to myself, either."

Giving her the honesty she expected from him, he admitted, "Yes, he reminded me of Toby. But I really don't want to talk about it, so let's go check out the cabin and breathe in some healthy Montana air."

They took a golf cart out to the cabin. The sun was absolutely brilliant in a perfectly blue sky. The mountains angled to the horizon. Wind pulled tendrils of Erika's hair free from her ponytail as Dillon glanced at her. The golf cart had more power behind it than he expected. It was great to be outdoors again, but it was even better to have Erika beside him, her arm brushing his, her smile as much of a balm to his soul as the sunshine.

When they came to a fork in the road, she directed him up a hill toward a grove of pines. Their scent rode the air and he almost felt as if he were driving into a forest. Soon the paved road gave way to packed gravel and stone. The cart jostled them as he drove at a lower speed. About a mile into the pines he caught his first glimpse of the cabin.

"Nice," he remarked as they climbed out and stepped onto the flagstone walkway leading to the steps and the porch.

Erika suddenly stopped and turned to study him. "Do you have a house in Texas?"

"I used to."

"You had the house when you were married?"

This was another subject he didn't really want to discuss. But he and Erika had reached a level where he had to if he wanted their bond to grow stronger. "It was a nice house, bigger than D.J.'s. I thought we rattled around in it, but Megan liked all the rooms and she said—" He stopped abruptly.

"What did she say?" Erika asked softly, as if she knew she was treading on sacred ground.

"She said Toby needed room to roam. I often wish—"

Erika waited.

"That I had played hide-and-seek in those rooms with him. That I could describe every one of his toys and exactly how he played with them. That I knew his preschool friends and the differences between them and which ones he particularly liked."

"Dillon, don't."

"Don't what? Beat myself up because I was a lousy father?"

"What would you have done differently?"

That stopped him cold because he had never asked himself that question. "I didn't have to become a doctor. I had a wife and a child and an oil fortune behind me."

"But since your dad died your mission in life was to become a doctor. Isn't that what you told me?"

"Maybe I should have changed my mission."

"And maybe you can't stop fate. Maybe you can't change the hand you're dealt, no matter how much you want to. Do you think if you hadn't become a doctor, if you hadn't been involved in your practice, Toby wouldn't have gotten sick?"

It was hard to hear his son's name on Erika's lips, yet he liked the fact she wasn't afraid to talk about his son with him. Did he believe that if the course of his life had been different the course of his son's would have been different? He knew that wasn't true. So why did he want that burden on his shoulders?

Erika must have seen the tumultuous thinking process her questions had stirred up, because she suddenly wrapped her arms around him, hugged him and said, "I didn't mean to start this here. I'm sorry."

The hug was meant to be comforting. However, when his arms surrounded her, when she lifted her face to his, comfort took on a different meaning. With their bodies pressed tightly together, he didn't want her comfort—he wanted her passion. His lips came down hard on hers. He kissed her possessively, deeply, knowing exactly what he wanted and hoping she wanted the same. The kiss that had begun with words, questions, pain and desire shifted and turned, becoming alive…becoming need…becoming hunger that had been pent up too much for too long. He tore his lips from hers, staring down at her, hoping to see what he wanted to see.

Her breathing was as ragged as his and just as shallow. "Let's go inside," she said, then took the key to the cabin from her pocket and handed it to him. He gripped it, clasped her hand, then walked up the porch steps with her.

The window in the door was a beautiful, thick, beveled glass that Dillon hardly noticed. After he inserted the key into the lock, his gaze was on Erika's.

When they stepped into the entryway, Dillon saw they'd really entered a small house, rather than a cabin. Everything was the quality Thunder Canyon Resort boasted of—terra-cotta tiles, handcrafted cabinetry, a native-rock fireplace extending from the floor to the ceiling. They'd entered the foyer between the kitchen and the living room and he could glimpse the doorways to the two bedrooms beyond.

After closing the door, he tugged Erika into his arms again, kissed her forehead, her cheeks, her neck. She slipped her hands under his suit jacket and held on to him.

"I know what I want," he said. "How about you?"

"I want you to make love to me."

He breathed a sigh of relief. "I'm so glad you said that."

She laughed. "Maybe I knew this would happen when I asked you to come here to have lunch with me."

He swung her into his arms and carried her into one of the bedrooms. The look was meant to be rustic but the lavish wine-colored comforter, the Tiffany lamp, the finely crafted furniture was more luxurious than fit for a cabin. Not caring about anything as mundane as decor when he had Erika in his arms, Dillon carried her to the side of the bed.

As he discarded his suit jacket, the most practical,

realistic thought hammered his libido. "Are you on birth control?" he asked her.

She frowned and looked so disappointed. "No, I'm not. I haven't needed to be. Oh, Dillon. You don't have a condom in your wallet?" she asked with an attempt at wry humor.

"No, I don't," he admitted. "I don't sleep around. In fact—" He stopped.

"Have you been with anyone since your divorce?" Erika asked gently.

"No."

The word hung in the room like a pronouncement that was too hard to take in. Then he reached out to her and ran his finger slowly over her lips. "We can pleasure each other without putting you in danger of getting pregnant."

Her beautiful, huge brown eyes searched his face and he knew she was trying to decide whether she could trust him or not. Could she trust him to keep her safe, not only from pregnancy, but from the hurt and pain of a short affair? He didn't know what might happen between them. He couldn't reassure her that everything would be all right. She had to make this decision on what she knew about him, and what they had right now.

She reached up and tugged open his tie. "The bed looks comfortable. Maybe we should try it out."

His heart pounding against his chest, he pulled back the covers and they lay on the king-size bed. His gaze wandered up and down her body. Her suit jacket was open and his hand came to rest on the silky blouse underneath. She rolled toward him, and began unbuttoning his shirt. They didn't seem to need any words as Dillon let his fingers stray toward her breasts, and Erika softly moaned as if she were eager to have him touch her.

So he did. He was rewarded by a soft sigh, a smile and the dance of her fingers underneath his shirt. He'd barricaded his heart for so long that he suddenly realized intimate touching between them could connect them emotionally as well as physically. Was he ready for that? Was she?

"Erika?" It was a question.

Her thumb found his nipple, circled it and skidded over it. He was so aroused he couldn't think. Yet he held on to rationality until she answered his unspoken question.

"I just want to be with you," she breathed.

As they removed each others' clothing, he found Erika to be a bit shy. She whispered, "I have a stretch mark."

He kissed it, looking at it, making her restless. "That's a memento of Emilia's birth."

He insisted on keeping on his briefs. He insisted on touching *her* everywhere, because that would be safer for both of them. When his fingers slid inside of her, she arched up and cried his name. Making sure her pleasure wasn't just momentary, his thumb glided over her most sensitive spot and she cried out again, her face flushed, her body awash in sensation and pleasure.

As she floated back to earth, he nibbled her neck and she wrapped her arms around him. "I want to do that for you, too," she said.

But he shook his head. "No."

"Just let me touch you," she whispered.

He felt as if they were doing something forbidden and dangerous and therefore even more exciting. He let her fingers roam over him, stroke him, almost send him to heaven.

Suddenly, he closed his hand over hers and brought it

to his chest. "When we can really *be* together, you can touch me all you want."

When he kissed her again, he showed her how much he wanted her, imitating with his tongue exactly what he wanted to do with his body. Her hands delved into his hair, and her kisses returned his fervor.

When they stopped to catch their breath, he rolled over on his back. "I could stay here with you like this all day. But I have to get back."

"I know." Her voice sounded sad and wistful. Then she propped up on her elbow. "Thank you, Dillon."

"For what?"

"For not trying to take advantage of me."

"You're welcome," he said simply, glad she was finally learning who he was, pleased she was trusting him.

Erika's gaze slid over his body and saw that he was still aroused. She blushed. "I think there are spare sheets in the closet. I need to change these."

She had her back to him now as she dressed, and he wondered if their make-out and petting session had unnerved her as much as it had unnerved him. He knew it raised a question in both their minds. What was next? Neither of them exactly knew the answer to that.

He climbed out on the other side of the bed, found his clothes and was dressed before she'd finished buttoning her blouse. "You wanted me to let you know what Zane might like here. He'd prefer the temperature to be kept down. He likes to light a fireplace. He takes his coffee black and drinks gallons of it, so stock up on that. And stock the refrigerator with bacon and eggs. He'd rather make his own breakfast instead of waiting for it to come from the resort. You also might want to put a chair out on the front porch. He often watches the sunrise."

She undid her bun which had almost come undone and ran her fingers through her hair. "You do know him well. Does he know you as well?"

"He probably does. We haven't spent that much time together lately. But we did once."

"Did you push all of your friends away after Toby died?"

Sometimes she absolutely unsettled him. "I guess after something traumatic happens in our lives we can either reach out for support or push everyone away. I pushed friends away. I needed Megan's support. But we weren't there for each other. Too much had happened before, during and after. At that point she wanted someone to blame. I was a doctor so she blamed me."

"But it wasn't your fault. You have to know that."

He didn't respond. "I guess it's natural to look for someone to blame when something so important goes wrong."

"I blamed Scott at first when Emilia was born. But then I realized *I* made the choices that got me into the mess."

"I did resent Megan because she didn't hold on after Toby died."

"What do you do with the old baggage?" Erika asked.

"I guess we try to learn from it and hope we don't make the same mistakes again."

She looked down at her hands rather than at him, and that was unlike her. Finally, her gaze lifted to his. "What happened here today scares me, Dillon."

"Because of something I did?"

"Oh, no. Nothing like that. It's just, except for Emilia, I try not to feel too much about other things. I try not to get too attached in case they slip away. Today with you I felt a *lot*."

Crossing to her, he slipped his hands into her hair and tilted her chin up with his thumbs. "If you didn't feel a lot, I wouldn't want to make love to you."

"You still want to do that?" she asked lightly.

"Oh, yeah."

As if the intensity of the moment was too much, she looked away from him and checked her watch. "Oh, my gosh. I'd better get those sheets."

"I'll help you make the bed," he assured her, and laughed when she looked surprised. "I do great military corners."

"But you weren't—"

"In the military? No. But my stepdad was, before he worked on the oil rig."

"There's so much about you I still don't know," she said as if that bothered her a great deal.

"The more we're together, the more you'll learn."

He saw the flicker of hesitation in her eyes, the reluctance to believe they could have a future.

A short time later, Dillon walked beside Erika into the lobby of the lodge. What he wanted was to pull her into his arms and kiss her again. And every time she glanced at him, he thought she wanted to do the same thing.

In the lobby someone called Erika's name. Dillon saw the woman at the counter beckoning to Erika. "Go ahead," he said. "I'll make sure everything is quiet in the infirmary."

Erika's gaze lingered on his face. She probably wondered what he was thinking, just as he wondered what she was thinking. Then she broke away from him and headed for the desk.

As Dillon went down the hall and into the reception area, he noted it was empty. Ruthann was in her office, typing information into the computer.

He stopped at her doorway. "Thanks for covering over lunch."

"No problem. All was quiet. I understand the need to escape from here every once in a while. The resort can begin to feel like a prison. Especially when you're on call day and night."

"Well, we'll both have free time this weekend when Dr. Babchek covers. Are you going to sample chili and listen to the campaign speeches?"

"Arthur Swinton has been around for a long time. I know what he's going to say. He spouts off to the town council whenever he gets a chance. But Bo Clifton? That could be interesting."

Before Dillon had a chance to comment, his cell phone chimed. Taking it from his pocket to check the caller ID, he was surprised to see his stepfather's name. "Excuse me," he said to Ruthann. She nodded as he went to his office and closed the door.

"Hello, Peter," he answered. "What can I do for you?"

"I just thought I'd check in. With a job at a resort I thought you might be having a massage or off hiking on the trails."

Dillon's hackles rose and he told himself the best thing was just to stay silent.

After a few moments, Peter cleared his throat. "Just making a joke. I know you're working hard there. You always do. It's your nature."

Yes, it was his nature. Did Peter actually know that?

Did he know *him?* Dillon had always thought that, since he'd detached himself from Peter, his stepfather wouldn't see things. But detachment didn't make a person invisible. "This is a different kind of practice than I'm used to."

"I imagine so. You might even have children to treat."

Peter wasn't asking but he *was* probing. Had his mother told him to? After her first few attempts to discuss Megan and Toby with him, she had seen Dillon was shut down on the subject. But now time had passed and maybe she had told Peter to have a go at it.

Making an attempt to relate to his stepfather, knowing his mom would appreciate that, Dillon replied, "I did have a couple of children to treat. One was an eight-year-old with an allergic reaction to something he ate. It was quite serious but we turned it around."

"Really?" Peter seemed surprised he'd discuss it. "Did you…handle it okay?"

"I didn't have time to think about anything but the emergency." He thought of Emilia and how he was attempting to deal with the idea of getting involved seriously with her and her mom.

"Did you decide whether or not you're going to join the concierge practice?"

"No, I haven't decided. I've been weighing all my options." His conversation with Erika at D.J.'s had planted a new idea in his mind. "Actually, I was considering using some of that oil money I inherited for a free clinic. If not that, maybe doing a stint of volunteer work somewhere."

"That's a substantial change. You'd really do that?"

Again Dillon went silent, not knowing if his stepfather had thought he was driven, shallow or simply not altruistic. Dillon knew he'd been self-absorbed in med school and when he'd joined the practice. That was one of the reasons his marriage to Megan had faltered. It was one of the reasons he hadn't had the relationship with Toby he should have had. Now in some ways everything seemed clearer.

Dillon could hear Peter let out a long breath. Then his stepfather said, "The money is yours to use as you want. Your dad would be proud of the way you've invested it well. *I'm* proud. Not only of the way you've handled the money, but of the man you've become. I know that might not mean anything to you coming from me—"

"That's not true," Dillon cut in. "It does mean a lot." In fact it was the first time he'd heard his stepfather say anything like that. Then again, when had he given him the chance?

"Well, good. Your mom's proud of you, too. I'm sure you'll give a lot of thought to whatever you choose to do. Your mom sends her love. She said she'll call you soon. She wants to know the best time."

"Evenings are good."

"I'll tell her that. Take care, son. I'll see you when you get back to Midland."

Dillon said goodbye to Peter and closed his phone, the word *son* still echoing in his mind. He suddenly realized the wall he'd built between himself and Peter all those years ago might finally be falling down.

When Erin Castro beckoned Erika over to the receptionist's desk, Erika didn't know what to expect.

"Do you have the cabin ready for Zane Gunther?" her friend asked.

"You want a backstage pass, don't you?" Erika asked with a smile. Erin was a huge Zane Gunther fan, too.

She'd talked to Zane's manager about those and she could get about ten of them.

"I'd love one. Will I really be able to meet him?"

"It's called a meet 'n greet. You'll probably have about three minutes with him and you can have your picture taken."

"I can't wait for Saturday night. His concerts are supposed to be the best." Erin hesitated a moment and then said, "I saw you come in with Dr. Traub. Did you two have lunch together?"

Actually they'd forgotten all about lunch. Something must have shown on her face because Erin asked in a low voice, "Are you two involved?"

Erika liked Erin and they'd had a pleasant lunch together last week. But she didn't want to reveal too much. Employees talked, though Erin seemed as isolated sometimes as Erika herself did. "Not exactly involved."

"I heard he has lots of brothers and sisters. Is that true?"

Was Erin fishing? Just curious about Dillon? "He has four brothers and a sister."

"Do they all live in Texas?"

"I think so. Why so interested?"

Erin was quick to say, "Oh, I'm not cutting into your territory. I was just curious, that's all. I know he's Dax and D.J. Traub's cousin. But Dax and D.J. don't have anything to do with the oil fortune, right?"

"I'm not sure about that. But it was Dillon's father who was involved in oil."

"And he died," Erin filled in.

"Yes." Erika didn't feel comfortable going into more detail. After all, Dillon's private life was his private life. If anyone could appreciate that, she could. She changed the subject before Erin could ask her more questions.

"So, will you be attending Frontier Days or will you be working?"

"I'm off Saturday afternoon, and of course in the evening for the concert."

"Before I forget, Emilia's birthday is Sunday. Would you like to come to her party?"

"Sure. Will Dr. Traub be there?" Erin asked slyly.

"I haven't asked him yet," Erika admitted.

"Well, you can count on me to be there. Just let me know what time."

"Will do," Erika replied. "I'd better get back to work. As soon as I have the backstage passes I'll make sure you get one."

Erin impulsively gave her a hug. "Thank you so much. This means a lot."

Erika smiled, glad she and Erin were becoming friends. It would be nice to have an ally at the resort.

Yet as she hurried to the infirmary, she wondered why Erin had been so curious about Dillon. Maybe at Emilia's birthday party, she'd find out.

If she invited Dillon to the party, maybe she could figure out where they were headed. On the road to a romantic dream...or on the road to heartache?

Chapter Eleven

Erika checked the cabin one last time Friday morning, almost in a panic. Everything looked perfect. Zane Gunther's favorite foods were stocked in the kitchen. The scent of fresh lemon polish still lingered in the living room. But Dillon wasn't here yet, and he'd said he'd introduce her to Zane.

Since when had a man in her life ever done what he'd said he'd do?

Dillon is different, that little voice inside of her heart reminded her. But she was afraid she'd be disappointed again. She was afraid she'd be hurt.

Being in this cabin once more reminded her of what she and Dillon had done here. They'd become intimate in a way she'd never been intimate with a man before. It hadn't been about undressing and kissing and touching. The difference was the way Dillon had treated her...so passionately, yet so gently. The way he'd protected her, foregoing his own pleasure.

Yet still she had doubts. Had her father's desertion given her these insecurities? Or was Scott's desertion to blame?

Suddenly Erika heard the sound of tires on gravel and hoped Dillon was arriving. But then she realized the sound was the lumbering hum of a bus rather than a car. Leaving the cabin for the front porch, she spied a huge silver bus come into view. It rambled up the lane, and she felt excitement zinging through her veins. She was going to meet Zane Gunther!

As the bus found a place to park under the trees alongside the cabin, another vehicle sped down the lane faster than it should have.

Erika expelled a huge sigh of relief when she saw Dillon had indeed arrived in time. Why hadn't she trusted that he would?

As Dillon strode up the walk, he extended his hand to her with a huge grin on his face. She saw he was almost as excited as she was.

Seconds later the door on the bus opened with a swoosh and Zane Gunther himself stepped out. She spotted a huge burly man waiting on the steps.

Dillon leaned close to her. "That's his bodyguard, Roscoe. He'll be close by. He goes anywhere Zane goes."

When Zane spotted Dillon, he tapped his Stetson harder onto his head and rushed forward to greet him. His green eyes sparkled with pleasure. The two men clapped each other on the back, each chiming in with "It's great to see you" and "Today was a long time coming."

Erika could tell from their enthusiastic greetings that

there was true affection between the two men. Then both of them were suddenly looking at *her*.

Dillon said, "This is the coordinator of Frontier Days, Erika Rodriguez. Erika, this is Zane."

She extended her hand to shake his. "Mr. Gunther, this is such a pleasure."

His grip was firm and strong. "Call me Zane, please. My manager said you're a pro at this."

"Hardly. This is the first time I've handled arrangements for someone like you."

Zane chuckled. "Honest, too. I think we'll get along just fine."

Erika was ready with one of her business cards, and she handed it to him. "If you need anything, anything at all, you just call my cell number. I'll be in town this afternoon, but if I can't get here myself, I'll send someone with whatever you need. Your manager said you wouldn't need a car." She looked at the bus. "Are you sure about that?"

"I'm sure. If I go anywhere, I'll just do some hiking. I don't want to raise a ruckus in town with a festival going on. Dillon knows how ugly that can get."

"We almost had our shirts torn off once," Dillon admitted with a wry smile that Erika felt in her belly. She was standing here with Zane Gunther, megastar, but it was Dillon who turned her on.

Struggling to maintain her composure, she said, "Come on inside. Make sure everything's to your liking."

Zane tossed another smile at Dillon, then went inside to check out his quarters.

Five minutes later he'd rejoined Erika and Dillon in the living room, his Stetson removed, his hand raking through his red-brown hair. "The cabin is great." He crossed to the cupboards and opened them, then did the same with the refrigerator. "Dillon must have told you what to stock up on."

"He did. I was glad for his advice."

Zane looked from one of them to the other. "Mmm-hmm," he said, and Erika wondered exactly what Dillon had told his friend. That they were a couple? Maybe that they were becoming a couple?

Zane was speaking again. "Roscoe will bring my gear in, then I'll get settled." He told Erika, "My manager will be arriving later." Turning to Dillon, he asked, "Are we still on for tonight? Some of that beer in the refrigerator has your name on it. And if we are—"

"Yep, we're still on. Dr. Babchek's going to cover for me tonight. I'll take over in the morning, but he'll be on call again tomorrow afternoon and evening. Grant's giving him a room in the lodge so he'll be on site."

Zane said to Erika, "My band was pleased with their condo. You can meet them all tomorrow if you want, if you decide to stop by at the sound check in the afternoon."

"I'd like that. I have to be in town for the mayoral speeches, so I'll drive over afterward."

"That sounds great."

Zane walked with them to the door and gave a shout to Roscoe. "Bring it on in. I'll get the guitar. See you later," he called to them both as he ran to the bus.

Dillon took Erika's hand and walked her to her car.

"He *is* just a regular guy," she said with surprise.

"Always was, always will be." As Dillon's gaze held hers, her heart started racing in a different way than it had with the excitement of meeting Zane Gunther.

"So," Dillon drawled, "I happen to be free tomorrow

afternoon. I can go with you to the speeches and stop in on the sound check with you if you'd like."

"I'd like," she said with a smile, knowing he wanted to kiss her, knowing she wanted to kiss him. Yet they still weren't free enough with each other to just do it. Because they both still had doubts?

"Let me take you to the concert tomorrow night. We can spend some time together afterward." He paused. "In my suite." Obviously not wanting to pressure her he gently added, "You don't have to decide now. Think about it."

What he was asking almost took her breath away. Did she want to take the leap of spending the night with him?

"I'll think about it," she promised him.

"Good luck with the start of the festival today. And everything tomorrow." His smile slowly faded away. "I'd like to spend time with you tonight, but I supposed you wouldn't want to be away from Emilia two nights in a row."

He was talking about the concert. He was talking about her spending tomorrow night with him. "I'm glad you understand." As soon as she said the words she knew she shouldn't have. Of course he understood. He'd been a father, too. She saw the cloud across his face, the pain darken his eyes. How could he ever get close to Emilia when he was still recovering from the loss of his son?

Dillon dropped his hand from her face. Their lighter conversation had turned very serious and she could feel him withdraw.

Roscoe's booming voice sailed to them across the yard as he said to Zane, "Nice place for a stopover."

"You've got an apartment on wheels all to yourself,"

Zane quipped. "What are you complaining about?" Roscoe's laugh was as loud as his voice.

Dillon said, "I've got to get back and make sure everything is in order for Dr. Babchek when he arrives later. You're heading into town?"

She nodded, sorry they'd lost the connection that had been there just moments earlier. "I'll call you later," she said, trying to regain it.

But Dillon just waited for her to get into her car, then he climbed into his. He drove down the lane, leading the way.

If she stayed with him tomorrow night, would that be the biggest mistake of her life—or the start of their future together?

On Saturday afternoon, as Erika worked her phone, made sure the microphone in the town square was functioning properly and consulted with other employees of Thunder Canyon Resort whom she'd delegated detail work to, she couldn't erase her conversation with Dillon from her mind. She couldn't forget the look on his face when he thought about his son. She couldn't even imagine the pain she'd feel if something happened to Emilia.

She glanced toward the campaign tents that were set up on the square's grassy area, one for Bo Clifton and one for Arthur Swinton. All of a sudden she recognized the man striding toward Bo's tent and her heart skipped.

Dillon.

He looked so sexy in a football shirt and jeans, his Stetson tilted over his brow. Broad shouldered and long waisted, he'd stand out in any crowd. She watched him approach Marlon Cates and his fiancée, Haley Anderson.

Grant was there, too, a stack of campaign brochures for his brother in his hand. Connor McFarlane, who a couple of months ago had been rumored to be thinking about buying out Thunder Canyon Resort, had his arm around his fiancée, Tori Jones, a teacher at Thunder Canyon High School. She was speaking to Allaire, and D.J. was in conversation with Dax.

Erika's gaze returned to Dillon just as he looked up onto the platform where she was standing. The whole town square seemed to vibrate with the attraction that kept pulling her closer to him. Her longing and need to find happiness with Dillon was so intense it was making her tremble. She knew she had to trust to find happiness. She knew she had to make a decision about tonight. When she'd asked her mother last evening if Emilia could stay with her tonight because she might be very late getting in, her mom had said at once of course Emilia could stay. But she'd looked worried and concerned, as if she knew exactly what Erika was really planning.

Not that she had come to a decision yet. But maybe the rest of the day could help put her life in perspective…could help put her relationship with Dillon in perspective.

The crowd was thicker now. Bo was going to make a dramatic entrance instead of just walking up the steps to the platform. His campaign manager, Rose Friedel, would be introducing him. Erika's work here was finished for the moment. She made her way to Dillon, unsure how he'd greet her after his withdrawal and quick departure yesterday. Is that how he'd leave Thunder Canyon, too? Quickly, without a second thought for her or Emilia?

Shoving those disturbing thoughts into the back of

her mind, she approached him with a smile. He smiled back and her world shook again. She didn't want to be an easy conquest or a quick affair. She didn't want to have her heart broken. But she also couldn't deny this chemistry and connection to him any longer.

When she was within reach of Dillon, he dropped his arm around her shoulders. Although the brim of his hat shaded his face, she saw the simmering heat in his eyes. All she had to do was give a signal and he would kiss her. But it seemed as if the whole population of Thunder Canyon—plus every tourist at the resort—was gathered around them. There were employees from the resort who were doing her bidding, a couple of women and their families from her neighborhood, Dillon's family and friends. The whole gossip chain, just waiting to rattle.

So she didn't give a signal, and Dillon's hand simply tightened a little on her shoulder. "Everything looks great. You've done a good job." He motioned around from the red, white and blue banners on the grandstand, to the tents and refreshment stands and the booths along the street.

"I just did some of the organization. Did you and Zane have a good time last night?" She looked for signs that Dillon might have a hangover, but his eyes were clear, his jaw was freshly shaven and he looked rested. She remembered how Scott used to drink, sometimes after they made love. The next morning he would be blurry-eyed and sluggish, grumpy, too.

"We did," Dillon replied. "We talked until after midnight when Zane's manager arrived. We had a lot to catch up on."

And a lot of their past to relive? Erika wondered.

"Zane said he wrote a song that I inspired. He

wouldn't play it for me. He said I'd hear it tonight. It's going to be on his new CD."

"Most of his songs sound so very personal. Does he draw on real-life experiences for them?"

"Zane has a great imagination," Dillon said with a wry smile, "but yes, most of them are personal. Are you excited about the sound check?"

She was. But she had to admit she was even more excited about being with Dillon while they listened to the sound check. "I am. I have to remember to get back-stage passes from his road manager. He has a list from his fan club already signed up for the meet 'n greet." She shook her head, thinking about the planning that went into tonight. "And all this happens before the concert. Zane will be exhausted before he goes on."

"Not Zane. He loves to sign autographs and have pictures taken. It revs him up. He says he performs better when he personally knows the fans who are out there."

Dillon's hand was warming Erika's shoulder. She could feel the heat of his fingers through her suit jacket. She felt protected...cared for. Was that an illusion or real?

Allaire wound her way through the crowd to stand beside Erika. "Everyone really turned out. Did you do much advertising?"

"Radio, Internet, flyers and posters. Grant gave me a nice budget. The resort has many guests traveling here today just for the concert. A lot have extended stays to enjoy the resort. Even strangers have turned up here, interested in the campaign. But it's the townsfolk who count for votes."

D.J. came up behind Allaire and circled her waist with his arms. "Even Swinton's tent is overflowing. Bo might have the younger vote, but as the family-values candidate, I think Swinton has the couples over forty."

"We'll see what they both have to say," Dillon remarked, as if he had a stake in this election.

Did he? Erika wondered. *Was* he thinking about staying in Thunder Canyon? That was a question to ask him in private because she wanted to know if *she* was the reason he'd consider staying.

All of a sudden a cheer went up along the street. A buckboard pulled by two chestnut horses came rumbling toward the square. Bo was driving it himself.

"Smart image," Dillon said to Erika. "A man who controls the reins himself."

"Yes, it is. But I still don't know if a handsome young bachelor can counteract some of the old-fashioned thinking."

"Old-fashioned thinking might not help us out of this economic crisis," Dillon offered.

"That's true."

The crowd cheered again, until Bo's campaign manager quieted them and introduced her candidate with a short summation of his qualifications. "I'll let Bo tell you what he intends to do for this town himself. Come on up here, Bo."

Bo Clifton ran up the stairs with a vibrant energy that seemed to emanate from him. He was dressed in a Western-cut jacket, snap-button shirt, black jeans and belt with a silver buckle. His Stetson was tilted back, so his face and his very blue eyes were visible to everyone in the crowd.

"Hi, everyone," he said with a friendly smile that could easily earn a few of the women's votes. "I've come here today to talk to you about what this town needs for the future. Economic development—more businesses to locate their offices or plants here so we'll support more jobs. Better schools for our kids so they can become the engineers and scientists we need for the future. Better upkeep on roads so our cars don't break down every time we hit a pothole."

He received laughs on that remark and Erika realized this candidate just might have a chance.

Dillon had agreed to meet Erika at the fairgrounds arena at seven that evening, before the backstage activities and the concert began. He was afraid she'd feel she had to go back to the penthouse with him afterward if he picked her up. He had no intention of pushing her. Yes, he wanted her in his bed. He might want even more. But part of him was stomping on the emotional brakes. Was it seeing Zane again? Remembering his friend had been best man at his wedding to Megan? Remembering Zane had been godfather to Toby? Remembering Zane had been at the hospital with him and Megan that awful week before Toby died?

Stirred-up memories sometimes carried the worst body blows.

Just what good had talking done? The guilt and regret were still there. The pain wasn't ever going to go away. Not in this lifetime. His feelings for Erika were in turmoil at best. His desire for her, on the other hand, was alive and well. That was a physical fact as he caught sight of her walking toward him. She was wearing a form-fitting, Western-cut coatdress with fringes on the hem that met high boots. Her hair was loose over her shoulders, the way he liked it, held in place by a beaded barrette over her right temple. She was absolutely stunning, and his whole body told him he knew it and couldn't deny it, no matter how hard he tried.

She stepped right up to him and he playfully flicked one of her silver earrings decorated with tiny horses. "You look stunning."

"Thank you. You look quite handsome yourself."

Without much thought tonight he'd dressed in a gray shirt with a black bolo tie and black jeans. "Do you have your backstage pass?" he asked, joking.

To his surprise she slipped her ID from out of her purse and then another one for him. "Now we're official," she teased.

Settling his hands on her waist, he could feel her slender body under the dress. Oh, how he wanted to touch her. How he wanted to show her he cared about her. How he wanted to make love to her and find out what they were really all about. They were standing just inside the cavernous arena and no one else was around. Most of the people with backstage passes would have gone in one of the rear entrances. But Erika had wanted to get a view of the stage from the front, to make sure everything was perfect for the concert. Shortly, fans with tickets would start lining up at the door.

Dillon tugged her closer and was just about to bend and kiss her when the front door of the arena flew open.

Erika glanced over her shoulder and then broke into a smile. "Holly! When did you get back?"

Dillon didn't know the pretty young woman who was wearing a poncho over a flowing gauzy dress. He watched as she and Erika hugged a really long affectionate hug, almost like sisters.

Erika snatched Holly's hand and brought her over to Dillon. "Dillon, I'd like you to meet Holly Pritchett. Holly, this is Dillon Traub. He's been taking Dr. Cates's position at the resort."

Holly shook Dillon's hand, looking a bit embarrassed. "I didn't mean to intrude."

After a glance at Dillon, Erika said, "You're not. How did you know I was here?"

"I guessed you would be since you're coordinating everything. Dad got me a ticket for the concert and a pass to go backstage. He knew somebody who knew somebody. He knows *everybody*," Holly said with a sigh. Then she added, "When I drove into the parking lot I saw you coming in here. And I, uh…wanted to talk to you. I know this is a bad time but I thought maybe we could set something up."

"Sure we can. In fact—" again Erika glanced at Dillon and he wondered what that was about "—I'm having a birthday party for Emilia tomorrow evening. Come over about five. We can talk then."

"That sounds great." Holly looked toward the stage. "I can't wait for this concert, not to mention having my picture taken with Zane Gunther. I'd better hurry up and get backstage." Then with a wave, she left Dillon and Erika in the arena and exited as quickly as she'd come in.

Dillon didn't know what to make of everything he'd just heard, so he waited.

"Holly and I met when her dad was buying real estate," Erika explained. "He'd bring her along to the office. She asked a lot of questions about my job and we became friends. She just graduated from college in May. But she's been out of town the past couple of weeks, visiting a cousin."

"I see," Dillon said, still waiting. Erika fingered her ID card, then glanced up at him. "I guess you're wondering why I didn't mention Emilia's birthday party."

"That's one of the things I'm wondering about."

"It will be mostly women. Mom, a friend from work, Erin Castro—I don't know if you know her—a few women from the neighborhood."

"I can see how you'd think I wouldn't fit in."

"No, it wasn't that. I just didn't know if you'd want to come. I guess I didn't want to put you in the position of having to refuse."

As Dillon studied her, he searched for the truth. Her worried brown eyes told him she was sincere. "Why did you think I'd refuse?"

"Because I didn't know if you'd want to be around Emilia and the other moms with their kids."

"I was around Emilia at D.J.'s. I even helped you put her to bed Saturday night."

"I know. But every time you're around her, or other children, I see this look in your eyes. Being around them hurts, doesn't it?"

He closed his eyes and blew out a breath. "Am I so easy to read?"

"No." Then she corrected herself. "Well, maybe to anyone who cares about you."

He caressed her cheek. "You care about me?"

"Yes, I do."

"I'll be as honest about this as I can. Being around Emilia causes both happiness and hurt. They don't cancel each other out, they're both just there. I think I have to learn to live with that. But that doesn't mean I don't want to be around her. Now on the other hand, if you want to make it strictly a hen party, I understand."

After she gave him a thoroughly assessing look, she asked, "Do you think Allaire and Shandie would come if I asked?"

"I can't speak for them, but go ahead and ask."

"If D.J. and Dax would tag along, you wouldn't feel so lonely there."

Dillon laughed. "The three musketeers and a brood of women. That might work."

She punched his arm. "Seriously, I'd like to get to know Allaire and Shandie better."

"Then ask them. And if you want me there, I'll come whether Dax and D.J. attend or not."

This time when Dillon brought her close for a kiss, it was quick but thorough and almost made him forget she had a child who could bring him pain.

An hour and a half later Erika and Dillon sat in the front row of the arena, only a few feet from the stage. Erika had marveled at how many people Dillon had known when they'd gone backstage, considering he only visited Thunder Canyon now and then. When they'd come into the arena to take their seats, he'd waved to Melanie and Russ Chilton, then to Mitchell Cates and his wife, Liz, explaining who they were. It seemed as if there were many happily married couples in Thunder Canyon.

Backstage, Zane had waved to both of them as soon as he'd seen them. He'd even given her a hug, thanking her for all she'd done to make this concert a success, as if Thunder Canyon was doing *him* a favor. If only he knew how much revenue this concert had brought in for the resort and the town. Lodge rooms had filled up in the past two weeks with the publicity about Zane—his appearance had even gotten the resort mentioned on *Entertainment Tonight*. Hopefully, tourists would come in droves for skiing in the winter.

Erika's thoughts fled when Zane's band ran out onto

the stage. Dillon leaned close to her, his breath warm at her ear. "From the looks of it you've got a full house."

"*Zane's* got a full house. He sold out in about ten minutes!"

When she turned her face toward Dillon, their lips almost met. The lights weren't altogether dimmed yet, and she should have felt self-conscious. But she didn't. She'd fallen for Dillon Traub.

She was in love with him.

That realization almost made her dizzy. She wasn't sure yet what that fact meant for her and Emilia. Did she have the courage to take their relationship to a deeper level? If she had sex with Dillon, what came next? What if it turned out that sex was all he wanted?

Her questions faded as Zane's band soon had everyone in the audience clapping in time to their rhythm. Erika found herself getting caught up in the excitement, settling into the beat, tapping her foot. Worry didn't seem to have any place here tonight. And when Zane Gunther appeared on the stage, his guitar slung over his chest, his Stetson high on his head, his smile broad across his face, Erika realized that for the length of this concert she could just relax and enjoy.

For the most part, Dillon was caught up in the music, too. She saw him make eye contact with Zane several times, as if they shared an inside joke. Clearly their childhood bond had lasted many years. Erika was sorry she had lost contact with grade school and high school friends. And even with those she hadn't...her pregnancy had changed everything. Her relationship with Holly had stayed steadfast, though. Her friendship with Erin Castro seemed to be deepening. Maybe now she knew the true value of friendship. Good friends wouldn't judge her. They'd support her. She suddenly thought of Allaire and

Shandie and the possibility of forging a closer relationship with them. That thought made her smile.

In between numbers, Zane spoke to the audience, making people laugh and call out their favorite songs. He definitely had that country charm. He gave his all when he sang, speeding up the tempo with an almost bluegrasslike tune, then slowing it down with one of his well-known ballads.

During one of the ballads, Dillon leaned close and took her hand. He said, "We'll have to try dancing to one of Zane's songs sometime."

Dancing with Dillon. She remembered the first time, recalling vividly how she'd felt in his arms. When he looked at her under the bright lights of the stage, she could see he was remembering, too. Her body heated from the smoldering desire in his eyes. She had to make a decision about tonight. Soon.

Zane's show lasted an hour and forty-five minutes. Her hands were sore from clapping. Her ears were ringing from Dillon's whistles. He knew how to have fun and she loved seeing this side of him.

All too soon Zane pulled his stool over to the mike and sat down, positioning his guitar on his knee. "This will be the last one, folks."

He grinned at the protests from the audience. "Well," he drawled, "I could be convinced to do an encore. But now I want to sing you a song that will be out on my new CD. You get a preview. This is dedicated to a buddy of mine who I think needs a little nudge in the right direction." His gaze met Dillon's for an instant, but Erika caught it.

Zane told the audience, "This song's title is 'Movin' On.'"

The band strummed into the melody and Zane started to sing.

Erika felt Dillon go perfectly quiet beside her.

The audience was pin-drop still as Zane's voice filled the space. He spoke about a man who followed a path that went in the wrong direction. He sang about a kick in the gut, a turn in the road, a new highway to explore. She felt Dillon's arm tense as his friend moved into the refrain: *Movin' on from the past. Movin' on from then till now. Movin' on from the heartache into the sunshine.*

Erika glanced at Dillon, needing to know what he was thinking as Zane sang another verse and repeated the refrain. She wanted to know if Zane's words were touching him the same way they were touching her.

The song ended.

The lights went dim.

When they came back up again, Zane was no longer on the stage.

Erika leaned close to the man she loved. "Dillon?"

When he looked at her, her heart skipped a beat. There was so much turmoil on his face that tears came to her eyes.

Suddenly everyone was clapping, trying to convince Zane to return to the stage. The audience rose to their feet, whooping and hollering.

Dillon stood, too. But he stood slowly, like a man who was torn between the past and the present.

Would he still want her to come to his suite tonight?

Chapter Twelve

Dillon walked with Erika through the lobby of the arena and outside into the night air. He should be able to breathe better out here. But he couldn't. The air around him still felt stifling.

He understood Zane had thought he was doing him a favor…thought he was supporting him…thought he was helping him by writing that song. It was a tribute to their friendship as much as anything else, and Dillon wished he could just see it that way. But the song's refrain played in his mind and he kept getting stuck on the pain and the heartache. Pictures played, one after the other, of his wedding day, Megan's pregnancy, Toby's birth. He'd held Toby minutes after he was born and he should have kept holding him. But he'd let him go because medicine had called.

Sure, he'd seen his son walk and smile. He'd seen him roll over and sit up all by himself. But he hadn't been there for the firsts. He'd been at early-morning meetings, pharmaceutical reps' lunches, late patient appointments. But there *were* no excuses now.

Erika turned to him then and he saw the conflict in her eyes. She was trying to decide whether she should stay with him tonight or not. They really were a pair. He certainly shouldn't be encouraging *her* when he was stuck in the past. Yes, he wanted her. Most nights all he could think about was their arms entwined, their legs tangled, their bodies joined.

But at what cost? Even if he moved to Montana, that didn't mean his past wouldn't shadow him.

"Zane's song upset you, didn't it?" Erika asked as they stood behind the door at the edge of the crowd.

"It shouldn't have," he said, not really wanting to admit it. "That song said what I already know. I *do* have to move on."

"You can't move on if you don't forgive yourself," she said quietly again, as if she thought he needed to hear it over and over.

"If that's what it takes," he muttered, "it's never going to happen."

She looked at him carefully. "You don't want me to come to your suite tonight, do you, Dillon?"

He studied the night sky...the shining stars...the blackness behind them. "It's not that simple. I *do* want you to come to my suite. But I have a question for you. What if tonight's all we have? Can you accept that?"

She looked away from him.

"It's okay, Erika. I understand why you can't just live in the moment. You have a daughter to think of."

When she met his gaze again, he felt their connection, the bond that had been developing. He also felt the heat of desire between the two of them that never seemed to abate. This wasn't the place to have this discussion, yet maybe this was better than somewhere private. Somewhere private they might give in to the desire and forget the logic. Out here they were thinking about the consequences, and that was a good thing. Maybe later, when he was in his bed alone, he'd convince himself of that.

Erika's cell phone sounded from within her purse. She looked torn.

He felt torn. "Go ahead and take it."

She dipped her hand into her purse and pulled out her phone. "It's Grant," she murmured, and said hello.

Dillon heard her side of the conversation and he guessed what it was about. When she closed her phone she said, "I have to meet Grant inside with the manager of the arena. We have a few loose ends to tie up. I was really hoping...hoping we could talk more."

Talking was really the last thing Dillon wanted to do. "I'll go back to the resort. After you're finished with Grant—I'll understand if you just want to go home to Emilia."

Erika's eyes were huge and shiny and he didn't want to prolong this for either of them.

Suddenly she stepped close to him, kissed him lightly on the lips, then turned and went back inside.

He took one look at the yawning darkness inside the lobby. She disappeared into it. Then he strode to his car, trying not to feel anything.

Traffic was heavy for Thunder Canyon, with everyone leaving the arena parking lot at the same time. Dillon found a back way to the resort and followed the line of locals that knew it, too. At the lodge he saw folks heading toward resort restaurants to enjoy after-concert suppers. He wasn't hungry. All he could think about was the conflicted look in Erika's eyes.

Tonight was supposed to have been different from all the nights he'd spent alone since his divorce. Different from the emptiness ever since he'd lost Toby. Dillon supposed a crowded elevator was better than one only holding three or four people who wanted to talk. He got lost in the back, heard guests' conversations about how great Zane Gunther's concert had been. Deep down he agreed, and thought Zane's new CD was going to be a hit.

Movin' on from the past. Movin' on from then till now. Movin' on from the heartache into the sunshine.

Finally he was in the elevator alone. He inserted the key for the penthouse floor and the elevator went up another level. He got out, went to his suite and closed the door behind him. Why hadn't he just acted as if the song hadn't affected him? Why hadn't he just put his arm around Erika and kissed her?

Because that wouldn't have been honest.

In his bedroom he stripped off his clothes, stepped into a pair of sleeping shorts and didn't bother with a shirt.

His cell phone chimed, and seeing Zane's number in the caller ID, he answered it. Zane asked, "What did you think?"

"I think you turned me inside out."

There was a pause. "I didn't mean to do that. I meant to give you a kick in the butt. And if you let everything simmer down, it might just be the kick you need."

"If we weren't such good friends, I might boycott your CD."

Zane laughed. "Yeah, well, maybe in the next life-time, because we *are* good friends."

"Are you back on the road?"

"Yes, indeed. The bus is rollin' along. We're headed

to Denver. You know how it is, one concert after another."

"But you wouldn't have it any other way."

"No, I wouldn't. The boys are callin' to me. I'd better
go see what they want."

"Take care, Zane."

"You, too. I'll see you when I see you."

Dillon set his phone on the charger on the dresser. He
was still staring at the phone, remembering the evening,
remembering Zane's song when he heard a noise at his
door. He went into the living room and heard the knocking. Dr. Babchek, maybe? No, he would have simply
called if something was wrong.

Dillon swung the door open and saw Erika. Nothing
could have surprised him more. "I didn't expect to see
you again tonight."

Her gaze fell to his shoulders, to the hair down his
chest, to the waistband of his shorts. "I know, but—I
had to come. Are you going to invite me in?"

He wanted to—but then he stopped himself from
hoping. What if she'd just come here to talk?

When he stepped away from the door, Erika came
into the room. He wanted to take her into his arms and
haul her into bed. "Why did you come?" he asked, his
voice a bit hoarse.

"Because I thought you might…need me."

He needed her, all right. He was getting hotter by the
minute with that need.

"Kiss me, Dillon," she murmured.

She only had to say it once.

He took her into his arms and kissed her with all
the turmoil and confusion and desire that had been
building in him all evening. The intensity of it didn't
make her back off. Instead, she wound her arms tighter

around his neck, responded to every thrust of his tongue, pressed against him with the same hunger he felt. A sudden urgency to feel skin on skin seemed to drive them both. He lifted her into his arms and carried her into his bedroom.

When he set her beside the bed, he reached for the buttons on her dress as she tucked her hands beneath the waistband of his shorts. Her tiny gold buttons eluded his fingers and he swore. She helped him with them, and in no time at all, her clothes were on the floor next to his shorts. He covered her breasts with his hands, reverently admiring her.

She moaned and then asked in a low voice, "Do you have condoms?"

"A whole box of them," he replied with a smile as his hands slipped lower, almost circled her small waist and then settled on her hips. He kissed her again, pressing her to him so she'd understand the rawness of his hunger and the depth of his need. When she wove her fingers into his hair, she was so tight against him he could feel the beating of her heart.

Seconds later they were in his big bed, touching and caressing and breathing hard. They had known only a hint of intimacy in the deserted cabin. Now they were discovering the real thing. He caressed her body everywhere, wanting to know it as intimately as his own. She seemed to want to do the same. The stroke of her hands brought him so much sensual pleasure he didn't know how long he could hold on. She splayed her hands across his chest, slid them around him to his back, stroked and teased and tempted as he was doing to her.

Knowing they were both near their limit, Dillon reached for the box of condoms, found one and let her roll it on. When he slid his fingers between her thighs, she opened to him, and at the same time, took him in her hands. He groaned as she stroked him.

He whispered into her neck, "I won't be able to last if you keep that up."

"Maybe I don't want you to last. I need you, Dillon, just as much as you need me."

He leaned away from her and saw that basic truth in her eyes. There seemed to be complete honesty between them, and he'd never felt connected to a woman like this in his entire life.

"I'm ready, Dillon. I want you now."

He rose above her, not thinking or analyzing or debating with himself about anything. Pleasure was what they both sought. If it was an escape, so be it. If it was more, he'd deal with that tomorrow.

When he entered her, he sunk in with the craziest sensation that he was coming home. His thrusts had her gripping his shoulders. Their skin glistened from the excitement they aroused in each other. He couldn't hold back the hunger he needed to be fulfilled.

Erika urged him on with her moans, her sighs, her gasps of pleasure. They weren't two people any longer. They were one—on the same journey, headed for the same mountaintop. He watched Erika, saw the glistening haze of desire in her eyes, saw her cheeks flush, felt her hands hold him tight as if she never wanted to let go. Their bodies rocked together, seeking the mutual explosion. When it came, they not only found the mountaintop…they found each other.

When Erika awakened, the sun wasn't up yet. Last night she and Dillon had shared something so magnificent she knew she'd never forget their lovemaking. But now she had to go back to her house because Emilia was waiting. She had responsibilities and a daughter to think of. And although she knew she was in love with Dillon Traub, she also knew their time together was running out. Their bodies spooned together, his arm around her waist. She felt protected and safe in his arms—she felt loved. But the feeling couldn't last, could it? Had last night been an escape for him away from his past? Or was she really important to him?

She began to slip from his arms but his grip held her in place. "Where are you going?"

"I have to go home."

"It's early."

"I don't want Emilia to wake up without me and worry."

"She's two."

"She'll know I'm not there and wonder why, even at two."

Dillon took his arm away and let Erika scoot on her back so they could look at each other.

"Do you have regrets about last night?" he asked, maybe expecting her to.

Erika shook her head. "No. Do you?"

"No. But last night was intense in a lot of ways and I want to know what you're thinking."

She was thinking she was absolutely, wonderfully in love with him. But she couldn't tell him that. She couldn't take that final risk. Not without knowing what his plans were. Not without knowing if they had a future.

"What now?" she whispered, feeling much too vulnerable. "I saw all the feelings rise up in you when you heard Zane's song. You were thinking about your wife and Toby and the life you once had. You were thinking about a son you'd never see again."

"Don't." His voice was strained...almost harsh.

"That's the problem, Dillon. You haven't wanted to think about it. But you have to if we're going to have anything. I have a daughter. If this is just an affair and we'll have another week of pleasure before you leave, so be it. Last night that's what I accepted. But if on the other hand we want to somehow be part of each other's lives, I have to wonder how Emilia will fit in. Can you look at her with joy? Or can you only look at her remembering Toby and feel regret?"

When Dillon was silent, that was an answer in itself. She moved away from him and sat up.

"Everything just doesn't fall into place because last night was great!" he concluded.

"No, I suppose not," she said with a sigh, wishing it had fallen into place for him as it had for her. Loving a man wasn't something she'd thought she'd ever let herself do again.

The quiet emptiness of the suite seemed to surround them as she slid her legs over the side of the bed.

Dillon hiked himself up and clasped her arm. "Erika, do you still want me to come to Emilia's birthday party later?"

"If you want to be there."

"I do."

"Will Dr. Babchek still cover for you?"

"I don't think he'll mind covering another few hours for me. He told me he's really enjoying room service, especially when he doesn't have to pay the bill."

"I hope Allaire and Shandie, Dax and D.J. don't mind being cramped. My place isn't really big."

"You forget they're just everyday people."

"I guess I do," she admitted. Dillon sat beside her on the edge of the bed, ran his hand through her hair and turned her face toward his. Then he kissed her, trying to make the rest of the world go away.

The problem was that the sun was shining in the windows now and Erika knew she had to face her world exactly the way it was.

Erika was nervous. Not so much about Emilia's party. Everyone was already sipping punch and eating. Emilia was playing with the other children and having a great time.

No, she was nervous about seeing Dillon again. After he'd had time to think about last night, what would he feel?

In the kitchen, setting paper plates and plastic forks on the table beside the huge cake decorated with Winnie the Pooh, Erika felt a tug on her elbow. She turned and saw Holly.

"Hi, there," she said enthusiastically, giving Holly a hug. "I'm glad you could come."

"I wouldn't have missed it. You've got a great crowd here. Everyone seems to be mingling nicely." She hesitated. "Do you have a minute to talk?"

Erika and her mother had made sure the dining room table was full of food. "Sure. What do you need?"

"I need some advice."

Erika hadn't taken a good look at Holly since August. Now as she studied her, she could see something was different, though she couldn't put her finger on what. Ever since Holly had come home from college she'd worn flowing tunic tops. That seemed a little odd to Erika since she knew Holly had a wonderful figure. Sure, some of the time she could go with the hippie look, but all the time?

"Advice about what?" Erika asked, both curious and wary.

"On being a single mom."

"Oh, Holly. You're pregnant?"

Holly's eyes glistened with unshed tears. She pulled at her loose blouse. "Six months along. No one knows. I've been able to hide it with these clothes, but not for much longer. Please don't tell anyone."

"Of course I won't," Erika promised, lowering her voice. "Who's the dad?"

"A guy from school. I thought I'd found my Prince Charming, but he…he's taking an appointment overseas, and he doesn't care about me or the baby. At least I don't think he does. Unless he changes his mind and shows up ready to be a dad. The thing is, I like the idea of being a mom. I just don't know how I'm going to do it."

"Have you told your father?"

"Gosh, no."

"I don't think you're going to be able to wait much longer."

"I know. But I have to figure out what I'm going to do first."

"What you need to do is hold your head up high and carry your baby with pride."

"That's what you did, isn't it?"

"I tried to. You have to decide what you want and live your life on your own terms." She gave Holly's arm a squeeze. "And remember, you have friends. I'm here if you need to talk or if you need anything else."

After Erika gave Holly another hug she saw Erin in the doorway. "Come on in," she said.

"I didn't want to interrupt."

"You're not," Holly assured her. "We're all finished with girl talk for now." Holly picked up a tray of hors d'oeuvres on the counter. "I'll take this into the dining room."

Erin came over to the table. "I just wanted to let you know Dillon arrived. But he said he's going to bring Emilia's birthday present around back."

"What did he bring?"

"I don't know. But I think if he really does have brothers, I'd like to meet them."

There was a quick, sharp rap at the back door. Erika hurried to open it, and when she did she had to laugh. "What is this?"

Dillon was holding a brown-and-tan plush horse that was about three times taller than Emilia.

"She can ride it," he said proudly. "It also neighs. But you might not want to push that button. She could be afraid of it."

"And why are you bringing it in the back?"

"I didn't want it to be the center of attention. I thought we could give it to Emilia after everyone leaves." He set the horse by the table.

Erika shook her head. "Uh-uh. It's your gift to Emilia. You deserve to give it to her during her party. You know she's going to love it. Go ahead and take it in."

At the counter, Erin picked up a bag of chips. "I'll refill the basket and try to make room for the horse," she said with a sly wink.

Dillon and Erika both laughed, looked at each other, then went quiet. Dillon peered around her and saw no one was coming their way. He pulled her over toward the corner at the pantry closet, away from the guests' view. "I have something for *you,* too."

"What?" She was genuinely puzzled.

He took a light blue velvet box from his pocket and opened it.

"Oh, Dillon! It's beautiful." *It* was a gold lo[...]
a diamond set in the center. "I can't accept thi[...]

"Yes, you can," he said, taking it from the b[...]
slipping it around her neck. He fastened it in th[...]
then turned her into his arms. "I wanted to give you
something to commemorate being together last night.
You can put a picture of Emilia inside."

Erika wasn't sure what to do. She wanted to remember last night forever—but she didn't know if this was
a beginning or an end. Did he want to give her this
present so she'd remember him when he left? Did he
want to give her a gift simply because he liked her? He
had money. He could give gifts. Did they always mean
something special?

"Dillon, when would I wear it? It's so pretty. I
wouldn't want to lose it at work."

"This is a necklace you can wear whenever you want.
It has a nice heavy catch and the chain's a solid gold
rope. I'd like to think of you wearing it all the time."

Her fingertips touched it. When she looked into his
eyes, she believed he cared. She believed he cared a lot.
Her arms circled his neck. "Thank you."

His arms circled her waist and he brought her close.
"You're welcome."

His kiss was slow and sexy and she wanted to drag
him upstairs to her bed. But this was her daughter's
birthday party and right now, that was more important
than her being with Dillon. She thought about the little
boy he'd lost, his regrets and his guilt. Maybe she and
Emilia could help to heal all of that.

Breaking the kiss she lowered her hands to his chest.
"Let's give Emilia her horse and see what she says."

Moments later they were making their way into the
living room, into the midst of people gathered there.

Emilia saw Dillon and ran to him.

He set the horse down in front of her. "Happy birthday, little one. What do you think of this?"

Emilia's eyes grew large. "Horsey."

"*Your* horsey. Come here. Let's see how it goes." He lifted Emilia onto the back of the animal and she took hold of the handles on the saddle. She pushed her little legs up and down in the stirrups and grinned up at Dillon.

Then she said, "Dr. Daddy! Horsey."

The room went silent.

Stunned for the moment, Erika didn't know what to say. But then she rushed to her daughter's side. "Dr. Dillon, baby. It's Dr. Dillon." She cast a glance at Dillon and wasn't sure what she saw in his face. He looked a little stunned himself.

"She's been around Max and Alex and Kayla and hears them calling their dads Daddy." Dillon assured her, "It's an honor for her to call me that, Erika. Really."

Erika's fingers went to the locket he had given her. She looked around and saw her mother watching. Her mom would notice the locket and have questions.

Right now, Erika didn't have any answers. Dillon had said it was an honor for Emilia to call him Daddy, but that didn't mean he wanted to be her dad.

Chapter Thirteen

On Monday at lunchtime Erika gazed into the mirror in the employee's lounge, fingering the locket around her neck. She hadn't seen Dillon yet today. All morning she'd been in town, thanking business owners for their cooperation with the resort for Frontier Days.

Last night Dillon hadn't been able to stay after everyone left Emilia's party. He had to get back to relieve Dr. Babchek. But before he'd gone they'd found a few more quiet moments. The way he'd kissed her—

She thought again about how Emilia had called him Dr. Daddy. He'd brushed away the faux pas as if it didn't matter. But it did to her. Was he ready for a serious involvement with her and Emilia? The locket told her he cared. They had to talk about it. Maybe tonight.

The door to the lounge opened and Erin entered. Two other employees from the front desk followed her. Checkout volume had been high today and extra staff had been assigned to the desk. Erika didn't know Trina and Carrie well, but she'd worked with them at reception before being assigned to Frontier Days and the infirmary.

Although Erin approached her at first with a concerned expression and a glance over her shoulder at her coworkers, she attempted to smile. "Congratulations on Frontier Days. The word around the resort is you rock!"

"Zane Gunther rocks," Erika replied, wondering why Erin's smile was forced. "I think he's the biggest part of the success of Frontier Days."

Sidling over to Erin, Trina opened a compact, then peered into the mirror, her gaze meeting Erika's. "You should take all the credit you can. I heard Grant has his eye fixed on you for guest room manager when this is all done. That is if you're still around."

Guest room manager? Erika had hoped for that promotion. Could the rumor be true?

"Why wouldn't I be around?" Erika asked, puzzled by the odd note in Trina's voice.

Trina and Carrie both pointedly stared at her locket. "Nice necklace," Carrie said, as if that were an answer. "I heard Dr. Traub gave it to you."

Erika's gaze swerved to Erin's. Could Erin have gossiped about her?

But Erin was already shaking her head.

"Oh, we didn't find out from Erin," Carrie revealed. "Word travels. There were a lot of folks at your daughter's party. Besides, everyone saw you with Dr. Traub on Saturday night. We know what's going on."

Trina added, "Yeah, a girl has to take care of herself. You've hooked up with a good one. Past the necessities, you won't even have to be concerned about your daughter's college fund."

Erika was too stunned to speak.

After Carrie applied makeup and dabbed on lip gloss, she concluded with an edge, "I bet you'll soon have the earrings to match that diamond in the locket."

Erin moved closer to Erika in support as if she wanted to say something but didn't know what.

Sudden tears came to Erika's eyes and she looked down at her purse, opening it and concentrating on something inside.

Finally Carrie and Trina finished at the mirror. With a last look at Erika, and a "See you later," they left the lounge.

As if all her strength had seeped out of her, Erika dropped down onto one of the stools at the vanity. "Is that what everybody's saying about me? They think I'm with Dillon because he can...take care of me?"

"They're just jealous," Erin told her. "You've done well here, from what I hear, and in a short amount of time. Trina and Carrie still check in guests, whereas you had a giant responsibility for Frontier Days."

"That has nothing to do with Dillon."

"No, it doesn't. But the jealousy does. *You* are the one he noticed. *You* are the one he's dating."

Erika's fingers clasped the locket again. "This locket... he gave it to me because we shared something special. It's not a sugar-daddy gift. I don't want someone to take care of me. I can take care of myself as well as Emilia. I've proven that."

Erin sank down onto the stool next to her. "Do you love him?"

"Yes, I do. But the truth is, I don't know how he feels about me. He was married. He had a little boy who died. I don't know if he's ready to jump into this relationship."

"But you are?"

Erika sighed. "Yes. But not because he'll take care of me."

"Then you need time to find out how Dillon feels."

"We don't have that much time. He'll be leaving at the end of the week."

"A lot can happen in a week."

Erika supposed that was true. She needed to cherish each day they spent together. She had to hope that Dillon was falling in love with her as deeply as she was falling in love with him.

Still the old insecurities nagged at her. What if he wasn't?

Frozen in place, Dillon stood in the hall between his office and Ruthann's, cell phone to his ear. "When did this happen? How long ago did Peter start having symptoms?"

Dillon hadn't heard tears in his mother's voice since a few months after his father had died. She'd been a rock since then, taking over the business, standing up for her right to love and marry another man. And now that man had just been transported to the hospital.

"This morning, about 5:00 a.m.," she responded. "But he didn't tell me about the chest pain right away. Men. Trying to be strong when they should be asking for help."

"But he's in the CCICU now?"

"Yes. They're still evaluating him! They've been evaluating him for hours. I'm supposed to have a consultation with the doctor later. But Peter could be dying in there. Can you come? I know you could get information

I can't shake out of them. And you understand all that doctor talk. Besides, you're my oldest and—"

Dillon didn't hesitate for an instant. "Of course I'll come. But I need to find someone to cover me here first." Babchek had covered him most of the weekend. Would he want to take on more? If not, maybe he could recommend someone else. "I'll be there, Mom, but I also have to book a flight out. I don't know if I can get there before tomorrow."

"Your brothers and sister are here. It's not as if I really need you," she assured him, her voice clearing, strength filling her words once more.

"You asked me to come and I will."

"I know you and Peter have never really hit it off. But he said the last time he talked to you, you seemed different, more accepting of him."

"We had a good conversation. I guess I've been realizing how happy he's made you. That's what's important."

"I don't want to lose him," she practically whispered.

"I know you don't. I'll be there as soon as I can. I'll leave a message on your cell phone when I figure out flight arrangements." He wanted to say, *Peter's going to pull through this. You'll be able to retire with him. You'll have years of todays and tomorrows.* But he couldn't say that. After all, he *was* a doctor. He knew what was possible and he knew what wasn't. Until he saw Peter's chart, he wouldn't know exactly what they were dealing with. In his office now he took out a pad and pencil. "Give me the name of his cardiologist."

His mother did.

"I'll give him a call and find out anything useful."

"Thank you, Dillon. I—" His mother's voice broke.

He gave her a few moments, then he advised her, "Go sit with Peter as often as you can. He needs your strength and support. A wife can make a big difference in a husband's recovery."

"I'll stick to him like glue," she said with determination. After a pause, she said, "I love you, Dillon."

"I love you, too, Mom."

When Dillon closed his phone, he thought about leaving Thunder Canyon so quickly. Leaving Erika...and Emilia. Last night when Emilia had called him Daddy he'd gotten a glimpse of what the future could be. He *was* ready for it. Was Erika? Did she trust him? Were her doubts assuaged that he wasn't a man like her father or Scott Spencerman? What would happen while he was gone? Would the bonds they'd established break away?

He didn't know how long he'd be in Texas. He did know he had to make quite a few decisions while he was there...about his career as well as Erika.

Still upset from the conversation in the employees' lounge, Erika moved through the central wing of the lodge to gather the Frontier Days posters. Trying to believe Erin's words that Trina and Carrie were just jealous, she struggled to compose herself as she went from floor to floor with the expensive locket swinging at her neckline, reminding her that she had accepted the gift. A gift that could simply be a token from an affair. Doubts assailed her concerning her relationship with Dillon.

Returning to the main lobby for the final placard, her arms full, she intended to take the elevator to the storeroom beside the underground garage. But Erin came hurrying over from the desk, looking worried.

"I heard something I think you should know," Erin said.

"More gossip?" Erika asked, frustrated by it all.

"No. I wish it was. One of the bellhops was called up to Dr. Traub's suite. His orders were to collect Dr. Traub's clothes and pack them in the suitcases in his closet."

Erin's words felt like a lethal blow to Erika's heart. For a moment she couldn't catch her breath.

"Are you okay?" Erin asked.

"No. I thought I'd have time to talk to Dillon tonight…that we'd have more time together this week."

"Did you have a date tonight?"

No, they didn't. She'd just assumed that they'd spend the evening together. So much for assumptions. "You're sure about this?"

"I was right at the desk when the call came in."

"I can't believe this," Erika murmured, the posters almost slipping from her arms.

Erin caught them. "Here, let me take these. Where do they go?"

"The storeroom downstairs. But I have to do it."

"I think there's something else you need to do right now. Go talk to Dillon."

Could she face him when he hadn't bothered to tell her himself? Was this the reason he'd given her the locket? A goodbye memento? Was he like Scott after all? For the past few weeks she'd begun to dream again. She should have known better.

Erika took a bolstering breath and squared her shoulders. "Thank you for telling me." With a nod, she left Erin at the elevator and hurried toward the infirmary.

As much as Dillon's leaving hurt, it would have hurt even more if Erika had found out after he was gone.

Maybe there had been a message on her phone and she hadn't heard it. Pulling it from her purse, she slid it open. No messages.

Had she been so very wrong about Dillon? The horse for Emilia, the locket for her—they must have been parting gifts and she hadn't even realized it. How stupid could one woman be?

Erika hesitated only momentarily in the reception area. This wasn't the time to waver. She unclasped the necklace from around her neck.

Clenching it in the palm of her hand, she headed to Dillon's office, hoping he wasn't already gone. He was on his cell phone when she walked in...without knocking. She wasn't going to wait. She couldn't wait. Her heart already felt as if it were breaking in two.

Dillon looked totally preoccupied with his call. When his gaze came to rest on her, there was something there she couldn't read. Guilt? Regret? Was that all he was going to feel?

"Everything's taken care of, Grant. Yes, I will. Thanks."

He closed his phone and his eyes dropped to the V of her neck where the locket no longer hung.

She extended her hand and dropped the locket to his desk blotter.

His voice was clipped when he said, "It doesn't look as if the chain broke."

"No, the chain didn't break. But I have to return it to you. I can't accept a token from an affair that isn't going anywhere. Obviously."

"Obviously?"

"You're leaving and you didn't even bother to tell me! This is all my own fault. I knew you were going to leave. I even knew the date—October first. Were we getting too serious? Did you get shook up last night? Or maybe you're just not ready to move on with *me*."

"Are you finished?" he asked, looking wounded.

Wounded? Why would *he* look wounded? "There's nothing else to say."

He looked down at the necklace and then back at her. "There's a *lot* more to say. But you're never going to trust me, are you?"

"Trust you? *You're* the one who's leaving. And you didn't even tell me."

He appeared to be counting to ten. He appeared to be angry or frustrated or a mixture of the two. "That's because I didn't *know* I was leaving until about an hour ago. I didn't want to call your cell phone because I wanted to talk to you in person. Apparently I didn't get to you in time."

Was he telling her the truth? But why—

He continued, "I'm going home because my stepfather had a heart attack. My mother thinks I can interpret what the doctors have to say and give her the translated version. She's scared. She's going to expect me to find a way to save him. Maybe I'll be able to, maybe I won't."

"Dillon!"

"You sound shocked. As if I couldn't possibly have a good reason for leaving. I can see now, Erika, you're always going to doubt first and ask questions later." He attached his phone to his belt and moved out from behind the desk. "Ruthann's coming in. She'll be here in about ten minutes. Dr. Babchek will be taking over the office until Marshall returns. I guess you'll have to get your orders from Grant as to what you do next. Since I couldn't get a flight to Midland tonight Dave Lindstrom is flying me down."

"Dillon, I'm sorry I jumped to conclusions."

"I'm sorry, too. Last night I decided I *am* ready to move on. But it looks as if you aren't. I've got to go, Erika."

He gave her one long last look before he walked out of his office, and out of her life.

Dillon stood outside the glass doors to his stepfather's room, wondering when this man had come to mean so much to him. Had it been the day Peter had walked his mom into their garden and renewed his vows after twenty-five years? The day Dillon had invited Peter and his mom into his new practice to take a look at the facilities and his stepfather's wide smile had sent a message Dillon hadn't wanted to hear? Or had it been the day of Toby's funeral when tears had rolled down his stepfather's face, too? Maybe Dillon's feelings for Peter had simply grown over the years because this man had been there year after year, looking out for all of them and they hadn't realized it. At least Dillon hadn't.

Just as he hadn't realized the mistake he'd made with Erika. His head had been filled with the crisis here. When Erika had walked in, he'd been trying to figure out how he could bring her home with him. But she'd taken off her locket, practically thrown it in his face, and his pride had taken over. He'd been hurt once before like this and he wasn't going to let a woman crush him a second time.

Right. Texas pride at its finest.

As soon as Dave Lindstrom's plane had taken off, he'd understood what a monumental mistake he'd made. Yes, his own history had come back to bite him. But in his moments of anger and disappointment, he'd forgotten

Erika's history. She had more than one good reason to doubt him.

Because he hadn't told her he loved her.

Because he hadn't told her he wanted a serious commitment. If Peter continued to improve, he could fly back to Montana at the end of the week and hopefully make everything right with Erika. He didn't want to do it on the phone. He needed to do it in person.

Peering through the glass at Peter again, he saw his stepfather was awake. He pressed the button for the door to open and went inside.

In his early sixties, Peter was an average-looking man with a receding gray hairline and thinning hair on top of his head. He still looked wan but better than when Dillon had first seen him after his heart attack.

"I understand the procedure was a success," Peter said with an attempt at a smile.

"It was a success if you listen to Mom and your personal chef and eat a healthy diet. Mom says she's also going to hire you a trainer to make sure you exercise. Fancy equipment alone isn't any good if you won't use it."

"She's just mad because she bought me a Lifecycle last year and I wouldn't get on it every day."

"What about now?"

"Now I'll do whatever she wants. I want to be around for thirty more years."

"At least," Dillon agreed and was embarrassed when his voice caught.

He was standing near the bed and Peter reached out and patted his hand. "Did I scare you, too?"

He looked his stepfather straight in the eye and told the truth. "Yes, you did. I didn't realize how much I'd miss you if you weren't here."

"Well," Peter said and then cleared his throat. "The wind seems to be blowing a new way between us. What's happened to you?"

"Maybe I've finally realized what's important."

"You realized that when Toby was diagnosed."

"I suppose I did. But when he died, my world fell apart. I hung on to medicine and not much else."

"We could see that but we didn't know what to do about it. When we talked last week, you seemed different."

"I met someone."

"Ah. Now I understand. She's the one?"

"She's the one. She has a little girl and that made me have doubts for a while. But I'm sure now. Only thing is I acted like a jerk before I left. She found out I was leaving that day and thought I didn't care. When she doubted what I felt..."

"That dang Traub pride. Your mom has it, too," Peter noted with some amusement. "When are you going to fix things?"

"Soon."

"Don't wait," Peter ordered. "Life's too short."

"I'll fly out after you go home."

"Go now. Don't take a chance on losing her."

"I wanted to make sure you're okay."

"I will be. You can always come back to visit and bring her with you."

The more Dillon considered it, the more he thought it was a good idea. "Tell me one thing. How have you kept Mom happy all these years?"

Peter considered his question. "I guess the simplest answer is that I try to put her first every day. And I make sure to tell her how much I love her. You can't go wrong if you do those two things."

"Thank you," Dillon said.

"For what?"

"For treating me like a son all these years even though I didn't act like one."

"I knew you'd come around," Peter said with a grin.

Dillon was glad he had.

Erika hurried down the hall of the hospital in Midland where Peter Wexler was being treated. She still wasn't sure whether she should be here or not. While driving her rental car here, her heart had raced and her pulse had pounded in her ears.

After Dillon had left, she'd sat at her desk and cried. Not because he'd left, but because she'd been too insecure to believe he'd leave without a good reason. She'd been sure she'd ruined everything. She'd picked up the locket he'd left on his desk, knowing now it meant the world to *her* even though it might mean nothing to him.

At the end of the day she'd gone home and talked to her mother. Everything had spilled out—

She could recall every word of that conversation now.

"Do you really love him?" her mother had asked.

"I do. I know I haven't known him long, but I have such a strong connection to him." Tears had come to her eyes again. "I *had* a strong connection."

Her mom had sat next to her on the sofa and studied her. "At first, I wasn't sure about your doctor. But watching him with you and Emilia and knowing what he's gone through, I believe he's a good, kind-hearted man. Going to his family like this in their time of need proves it. If you truly love him, you should go after him and not let your past come between you."

She'd thought about going to his condo and sitting there and waiting for him, but she'd done something else that had taken a little more courage. She'd called Allaire. She'd told her what had happened and Allaire had been willing to help. She'd given Erika the information she needed and here she was.

Now she was just hoping—

Outside of the CCICU cubicles was a wide and long desk. Dillon was standing there, conversing with one of the nurses. He was dressed in jeans and a football jersey so she knew he wasn't there in an official capacity. She approached him and stopped beside him. "Dillon."

His expression was incredulous when he saw her. Then a mask slid over his face. "Erika."

"How's your stepfather?" she asked, really wanting to know.

"He's being moved to the transition floor this afternoon. He did have a heart attack. A stent was put in place and he can have a full recovery...*if* he changes his lifestyle."

"I know I don't have any right to ask this, but can we go somewhere private to talk?"

He hesitated a moment, glanced around and motioned down the hall. The door to the waiting lounge was closed. He opened it, checked inside and then gestured for her to precede him in. Then he closed the door and stood in the middle of the room, waiting for whatever she had to say.

Swallowing hard, she approached him and stood before him. "I'm sorry," she said.

His expression still didn't change. She knew she was going to have to make herself totally vulnerable and that was so difficult for her. "I know this isn't an excuse, but before I learned you were leaving, two of my coworkers implied I wanted to be with you because of what you could give me. They implied that I just wanted someone to take care of me and Emilia. I started doubting myself...what I felt for you...what you might feel for me. So when I learned you were leaving, I *did* jump to the wrong conclusions. I thought you'd used me like Scott had. I thought maybe Emilia scared you when she called you Daddy and you weren't ready for that. I thought so many things that I regret now. Because I love you, Dillon. I would move anywhere to be with you. In these past few weeks I've seen who you really are. You're passionate, kind and gentle, and you really care about everyone around you. Before you left, you said I doubt first and then I question. Now I'm asking a question first. Do you love me?"

His answer seemed forever in coming. But his mask began to fall away as he said, "I realize what a risk it was for you to come here and to tell me all this."

Then he was smiling and wrapping his arms around her. "I was angry with you because you doubted us. But as soon as I was on the plane, I realized why. I hadn't told you what *I* was feeling. What I had realized. I love you, Erika Rodriguez. And I love Emilia, too. It did shake me up when she called me Daddy, but it was a good shakeup. Because I figured out I *am* ready to be a dad again."

Erika's heart overflowed with love for this man she'd been afraid she'd lost. "Oh, Dillon. I was so afraid I'd wrecked everything."

He bent his head and rubbed his cheek against hers. "You didn't wreck everything. You just threw it off track for a little while. I wasn't going to let you go. I was planning to fly back to Montana."

His lips took hers then in a kiss that was burning hot, hungry, ready for escalation without much provocation. He was demanding and she loved the excitement of Dillon wanting her...Dillon loving her...Dillon needing her.

After he broke away, he shook his head. "I think we should get married soon, don't you?"

"You want to marry me?"

He laughed. "Oh, yes, I want to marry you. And you don't have to move. I'm going to set up a practice in Thunder Canyon and establish a free clinic. Maybe you didn't quite hear me the first time, but I love you and I love Emilia. I want nothing more than to be a husband and a dad. You and your daughter have changed my life. *Will* you marry me?"

"Oh, yes, I'll marry you." Then she reached into the pocket of her slacks and pulled out the locket he'd given her. "Will you put this on for me? I promise I'll never try to give it back to you again."

He gently turned her around and fastened the necklace as she lifted her hair. When he'd finished, he bent and kissed her neck. She turned into his arms, lifting her face for another kiss, knowing she'd truly found her Prince Charming.

Epilogue

"We're planning the wedding for November in Thunder Canyon," Dillon told Corey, as he sat in Erika's living room, watching her balance Emilia on the horse he'd given her.

"Mom's thrilled she's going to have another daughter," Corey informed him. "How does Erika feel about joining such a big family? What did she think of us?"

Erika had met his family on her whirlwind visit to Midland. After two days they'd flown back to Thunder Canyon to be with her daughter...soon to be *their* daughter. "I think she's going to like having brothers-in-law and a sister-in-law. She seemed at home with them."

Erika nodded and smiled at him, indicating she'd enjoyed the brief time she'd spent with the people he loved.

"So how does Erika's mother feel about her daughter marrying *you?*" Corey asked.

"She liked the fact that I asked her permission. She's more old-fashioned than Mom. But I think she likes me. She's enthusiastic about the clinic and believes it's just what Thunder Canyon needs in these tough economic times."

"Did you find a space yet?"

"Erika's helping me look. She's been promoted to Guest Room Manager at the resort, but eventually she's going to be my office manager. We're going to stay here in her house until our family expands."

"Oh, ho. Plans are in the works?"

"Possibly."

Corey laughed.

"So…" Dillon drawled. "Since you'll be in Thunder Canyon in November on business anyway, how would you like the job of my best man?"

"Seriously?"

"Seriously."

"I'd be honored. Does this mean I get to kiss the bride?"

"Only on the cheek," Dillon warned.

"Okay. I get the picture. She's yours and you intend to keep her forever, though I think the two of you just want to live in Thunder Canyon so you get out of our family Sunday dinners."

"Actually, no. I miss them. And I think Erika and I will have to fly down every once in a while to join in. I want Emilia to know her grandparents and her uncles and aunt."

"Her grand*parents?*" Corey inquired, surprised.

"Yes. Peter and I have found new common ground."

"You're at peace with yourself again." Cory decided.

"I am, thanks to Erika and Emilia."

"Do you think Zane will sing at your wedding?"

"He said he'd like to, if he can work it into his schedule. He feels instrumental in everything that happened."

After the two men laughed at the pun, Dillon said goodbye to his brother. Going to his wife-to-be, he crouched down beside Emilia. He pushed the button that made the horse neigh and she giggled. Then she held her arms out to him and said, "Daddy."

He lifted her into the air and held her in one arm while his other went around his wife-to-be. "I'm the happiest man in Thunder Canyon," he told her.

"Just in Thunder Canyon?" Erika teased.

"In the whole, wide world."

Erika stood on tiptoe and kissed him lightly on the lips.

Afterward he whispered in her ear, "Later."

She whispered back, "Later."

Yes, later he would make love to her. Later, he would tell her how much he loved her. Later, he would give her the diamond engagement ring he'd bought for her and they'd plan their wedding and begin to plan their future.

November couldn't come fast enough for him.

* * * * *

Don't miss the next book in the new
Special Edition continuity
MONTANA MAVERICKS:
THUNDER CANYON COWBOYS
Holly Pritchett was always the perfect golden girl—
until she got pregnant and her baby's father flew the
coop! Enter Bo Clifton, a renegade rancher
who is running for mayor of Thunder Canyon.
When he hears of Holly's dilemma, he offers
her his hand in marriage—with just a
few strings attached...

Look for
WHEN THE COWBOY SAID "I DO"
by Crystal Green.
On sale October 2010
wherever Silhouette Books are sold.
And look for TWINS UNDER HIS TREE,
the next book in
The Baby Experts series
by Karen Rose Smith.

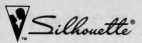

COMING NEXT MONTH

Available September 28, 2010

HARLEQUIN®

A Romance

FOR EVERY MOOD™

Spotlight on

Inspirational

Wholesome romances
that touch the heart and soul.

See the next page
to enjoy a sneak peek from
the Love Inspired® inspirational series.

*See below for a sneak peek at
our inspirational line, Love Inspired®.
Introducing HIS HOLIDAY BRIDE
by bestselling author Jillian Hart*

Autumn Granger gave her horse rein to slide toward the town's new sheriff.

"Hey, there." The man in a brand-new Stetson, black T-shirt, jeans and riding boots held up a hand in greeting. He stepped away from his four-wheel drive with "Sheriff" in black on the doors and waded through the grasses. "I'm new around here."

"I'm Autumn Granger."

"Nice to meet you, Miss Granger. I'm Ford Sherman, from Chicago." He knuckled back his hat, revealing the most handsome face she'd ever seen. Big blue eyes contrasted with his sun-tanned complexion.

"I'm guessing you haven't seen much open land. Out here, you've got to keep an eye on cows or they're going to tear your vehicle apart."

"What?" He whipped around. Sure enough, mammoth black-and-white creatures had started to gnaw on his four-wheel drive. They clustered like a mob, mouths and tongues and teeth bent on destruction. One cow tried to pry the wiper off the windshield, another chewed on the side mirror. Several leaned through the open window, licking the seats.

"Move along, little dogie." He didn't know the first thing about cattle.

The entire herd swiveled their heads to study him curiously. Not a single hoof shifted. The animals soon returned to chewing, licking, digging through his possessions.

Autumn laughed, a warm and wonderful sound. "Thanks,

I needed that." She then pulled a bag from behind her saddle and waved it at the cows. "Look what I have, guys. Cookies."

Cows swung in her direction, and dozens of liquid brown eyes brightened with cookie hopes. As she circled the car, the cattle bounded after her. The earth shook with the force of their powerful hooves.

"Next time, you're on your own, city boy." She tipped her hat. The cowgirl stayed on his mind, the sweetest thing he had ever seen.

*Will Ford be able to stick it out in the country
to find out more about Autumn?
Find out in HIS HOLIDAY BRIDE
by bestselling author Jillian Hart,
available in October 2010
only from Love Inspired®.*

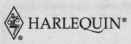

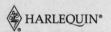

INTRIGUE

A MURDER MYSTERY LEADS TO A LOT
OF QUESTIONS. WILL THE ANSWERS BE
MORE THAN THIS TOWN CAN HANDLE?

FIND OUT IN THE EXCITING
THRILLER SERIES BY BESTSELLING
HARLEQUIN INTRIGUE AUTHOR

B.J. DANIELS

WHITEHORSE MONTANA

Winchester Ranch Reloaded

BOOTS AND BULLETS
October 2010

HIGH-CALIBER CHRISTMAS
November 2010

WINCHESTER CHRISTMAS WEDDING
December 2010